Cat and Buddha

David Walsh

Edited by Emily Heckman
Cover art by David Scheirer
Font by Rachel Lauren Adams
Graphic design by John McCloy

Luckydwalsh publishing.
Los Angeles, CA.

ISBN 9781980676041

TABLE OF CONTENTS

✧ one ✧

winter

Racing through the streets to escape a sudden rainstorm, a gray tabby cat comes to a halt at the spectacle taking place outside his home. In the curving driveway is a team of paramedics. Between them lies a covered body on a gurney. Is this who the tabby thinks it is?

The paramedics wheel the gurney into an idling ambulance, its emergency lights silently flashing against the wet cement. A static-filled voice speaks in short bursts over a two-way radio.

Tail alert, the tabby watches from under the trees as another group of uniformed men emerge from the house, this time carrying cages filled with frightened cats.

As the men loaded the cages into the back of an animal control truck, the tabby could hear the miserable howls coming from within.

One of the animal control officers approaches a woman dressed in a housecoat over pajamas. She stands watching the proceedings from under a dripping umbrella. The tabby recognizes her to be the daughter of the elderly woman he lives with. The officer produces a clipboard from under his arm and holds it out to her.

"Pet surrender," he explains, handing her a pen. She hastily signs the document then draws herself into her housecoat.

A wild dread courses through the tabby's body.

"Is that all of them?" one of the men calls out from the truck.

"That's it," answers another.

Instinct tells the tabby to keep out of sight. He backs into a flowering shrub, his green eyes glowing as he peers through the dripping leaves.

"These all the animals your mother owned?" the officer asks the woman.

She brings a fragile hand out from under her housecoat. "That cat there," she says pointing towards the tabby, "he lived with her too."

The officer turns and for a few awful moments locks eyes with the tabby. The tabby shoots through the hedge and disappears down the street. Two of the men make a motion to go after him then stop.

"That's all right," says the officer with a gesture of his hand. "I got a good look at him."

The tabby wasn't as far off as they supposed. Half a block away he had found a car to hide under.

Through the rain that bounced up off the pavement the tabby watches the men load the last of his housemates into the truck. It was as if he had never been truly alone until this moment. He blamed the owners he never knew, assuming they were the ones who left him in a box in front of a pet store. Luckily, he was taken in.

In the pet store, customers plucked every kitten from the kitten pen. Every kitten, that is, except the tabby. He despaired of ever being chosen. The owner also concluded that the tabby would probably never turn a profit for him.

"Something wrong with that one I think," he remarked to one of his employees as they passed a near-empty pen.

So he arranged for the tabby to be turned over to an elderly woman who had sparse silver hair and even more cats than the store. Indeed, judging from the meager portions of food she would leave out, she herself had lost count of her growing brood.

Feeling overlooked, the tabby took to the streets often, keeping the hours with the many diversions he'd found there.

In those days boys would try to lure him near in an effort to catch him, whistling and slapping their thighs as if calling a dog. But the tabby took pleasure in his freedom and kept his distance. Eventually, owing to how tatty he had become, the invitations stopped. The boys of the neighborhood assumed the tabby had turned feral and from that point on they were the ones to keep their distance.

Now, from underneath the car, the tabby watches the red taillights of the ambulance and animal control truck disappear into the wild night. He inches forward on his stomach out from his hiding place. Cautiously, he makes his way through the heavy rain back to the driveway.

The dark and lifeless house was evidence enough to convince him the covered body on the gurney was the elderly woman. This marked the culmination of his fall.

Memories of his lost opportunities float before him. If only he hadn't kept his distance when those boys tried to befriend him he might have had a safe place to sleep tonight. But he *had* kept his distance.

So it was that the tabby began his season as a stray.

✧ two ✧

the voice in the alley

The tabby wandered the streets with a heart as heavy as a stone, a pathetic figure in the rain. Away from all bright scenes he slunk, feeling he was good for little but to be laughed at. The world seemed insulting in its normality since tragedy laid its hand upon him.

And being at the mercy of Mother Nature in all her moods was the least of his troubles. In the days since the elderly woman had died, the tabby had been reduced to pulling scraps from the trash; so low was he brought.

Some days even scraps were not to be found and his dinner was limited to the tantalizing aromas that leaked from some kitchen window or local diner.

There was also the problem of other strays. Many cats he encountered had been on the streets a long time, some their entire lives. Most were hardened and cruel to their own kind. But most troubling of all was the animal control truck. The officer that saw him was intent on tying up the loose ends of his task. At least once each night the tabby was forced to hide as the officer's squad patrolled the streets of the city. The tabby knew it was only a matter of time before they would see him first.

It had now been fully five days since the tabby had lost his home. On this gusty winter's night, a night fit for extraordinary things, he found himself drifting into a back street, thick with the smell of garbage, beer and rain. After purging a waste-bin of its few fragments of food he lapped up some iridescent water that had collected in a breach in the pavement. He watched the widening rings that disturbed the water.

He had the distinct feeling the alley was not as empty as it seemed. He sniffed the haunted wind, seeking from it all that it could tell. He listened carefully. Hearing nothing, he returned to the puddle. "Trash and oily water…again," the tabby muttered under his whiskers. He grimaced from the disagreeable taste of the water when suddenly a strange voice rang out in the alley.

"*Watch the waves!*" it said, slightly foreign in its accent.

The tabby's ears pricked up tall above his head. Down he looked into the little puddle, then wildly about. He saw no one, which only increased his fear. The tip of his ringed tail flicked the greasy pavement, and before he was halfway through his next thought, he heard it again.

"*Watch the waves!*"

This time the disembodied voice made its way past the tabby's pricked-up ears and quivered down his spine. Every instinct told him further investigation would open a door to the unknown. His gaze wandered this way and that trying to detect the owner of the voice. "If you're talking to me, show yourself!" the tabby demanded, legs braced wide, waiting for what might happen next.

"*You have to look*," returned the voice, which seemed to be emanating from inside one of the waste-bins. The situation offered too much temptation so, being inclined by nature to curiosity; the tabby jumped up onto its rim and looked in. But the only things that met his eyes were waxen vegetable boxes, empty coffee cans and old newspaper.

"Where?" he asked.

"*You're looking at me*," the voice answered.

An unending procession of ants filed in and out of the bin. The tabby struggled to focus in on one. But as he moved close, the ants went so swiftly their individuality was lost completely and they looked for all the world like strands of black thread.

"Are you an insect?" he asked.

"*No*," said the voice. "*Do you see the little statuette?*"

After a moment of probing the darkness of the bin, the tabby singled out a small figurine carved in cherrywood, dimly visible amongst the rubbish.

"Yes," the tabby said, "what about it?"

"That's me," it replied.

7

"You can talk?" the tabby asked, bewildered.

"Fluently it seems," it answered.

The tabby had long held a theory that, given a sufficient length of companionless time on the street, a stray's inner monologue would mature into a dialogue. He worried his theory was no longer theoretical.

"Can everybody hear you?" he asked, looking round to see if there was another animal in the alley who could confirm this exchange.

There came the sound of someone opening a screen door. A busboy in a heavily stained apron emerged from the rear of a restaurant and emptied a mop bucket of its black water. The tabby hunched onto the rim of the waste bin.

"Hello!" the figurine shouted out. Wiping his hands on his apron, the busboy gave no indication of hearing the call and went back inside.

"Apparently not," the figurine concluded.

The tabby delicately stepped over the garbage until the whole of him was in the bin with the figurine. "How did you end up in here?" he asked.

"At one time I was a key chain that belonged to a woman. But I became a sore reminder of the person who gave me to her so she detached her keys from the top of me and tossed me into this bin."

The tabby asked the statuette if it wished to be removed from the bin.

"If it's not too much trouble," it answered.

Lifting his discovery from the bin, the tabby jumped to the ground with it. Placing the little wooden statuette at his paws, his eyes shone with wonder as he examined it from every perspective. On the figure's head, a tiny silver loop glinted. Crouching over, he put his snout to the figurine, which seemed the sensible thing to do. But it only made him sneeze.

"Gesundheit!" said the figurine.

The tabby stepped back, one paw lifted from the ground. "What's your name?" he asked.

"I'm afraid nobody has ever taken the trouble to name me," it responded.

"You look like one of those buddhas," the tabby noted. "I've seen pictures."

"Well then, for purposes of identification, I suppose you can call me Buddha if that's what I look like."

The tabby settled himself into a sitting position and confessed that he had never been given a name either.

"How about I call you Cat since that is what *you* look like?" Buddha proposed.

"You can call me Cat if you want," he said with a shrug of his shoulder. Then he asked, "Why were you saying 'watch the waves'?"

"The puddle you drank from—did you notice the waves you produced?"

Cat thought back, then turned his head toward the puddle. "I guess," he said.

"I can see that your tongue has that same effect on the air around you, through your words and thoughts. When you bemoaned your misfortune a second ago, I noticed that you produced waves of another kind. Ones that are adversely affecting your experience."

"I couldn't help it—that water tasted awful," Cat griped.

"That would seem to be a message from your body telling you to refrain from ingesting any more of it. Maybe your thoughts and emotions of a distasteful nature are no different in that they are a warning against their harmful repercussions."

"I just came here to find some food," Cat snapped as he jumped onto the rim of one of the untried bins. Then he deposited himself bodily into it and rooted through its contents.

"Could it be that you came here because you need me, and I happened to be put into the bin yesterday because I'd be needing you?" Buddha inquired.

As Cat flung rejected debris over the top of the bin, from the depths, he called out, "What would you need me for?"

"Perhaps together we will be able to find someplace nicer to stay than a garbage alley."

Cat reached the bottom of the bin and found nothing. He felt himself considering Buddha's proposal, for this life of scavenging had proved a bitter business. He reemerged from the bin and hopped down onto the pavement. "What nicer place?" he asked more earnestly now in spite of himself.

"I can sense that to reach it we'll have a bit of a journey ahead of us," Buddha informed him.

"Journey?" Cat repeated. "Why would I wanna do that?"

"Well, for one thing, you do not have much choice in staying with those men intent on catching you," Buddha said.

Cat started, and for an instant looked at him with wide-open eyes; then they faltered and fell. "How did you know about that?" he asked quietly.

Buddha continued, "What's more, you can finally fulfill your longing for a real home."

Cat well realized the futility of denial—his mere presence in the alley at this unreasonable hour spoke plainly to the fact that he was homeless.

Buddha assured him that together they could find a proper home. And though Buddha's proposal sounded like quite the undertaking, Cat had been praying for something better, whatever it might be. But not wishing to appear too gullible, he casually inquired as to the whereabouts of this nicer place.

"I can sense that we'll need to travel north," Buddha answered. "I'll have to leave the rest to you," he added ominously.

"To me?" Cat asked. "How do *I* know where it is?"

"Your desire for a home will lead the way, that same desire will lead you to the freedom you've been seeking as well."

"This is where my freedom has got me," Cat said, indicating the waste-bin by a nod of his head.

"That's not what put you here," Buddha answered.

"What then?" Cat challenged.

"I might be able to explain things to your satisfaction but I'd like to do it along the way if you don't mind," Buddha offered.

Cat was a long time in answering. He heard a single car passing by. Somewhere in the distance a dog started up a half-hearted bark, then stopped.

"I know you said north, but aren't you afraid we'll get lost. You don't seem to know any details," Cat said.

"As with all cats, details are only seen in hindsight," Buddha replied.

"In hindsight?" Cat asked.

"*Hind-sight, de-tails,* get it?" Buddha asked.

"Oh," Cat responded with a crooked smile.

There was a small silence. The wind swirled scraps of litter. The world waited.

Cat contemplated the alley with its broken bottles and filthy waste-bins.

He reflected upon the indignities he had endured on a daily basis. How often now, when seeking shelter near a human's dwelling, had an angry resident taken a broom to him? How often had he found himself engaged in vicious territorial fights with other strays? How much more rancid food must he eat?

And to crown it all…animal control.

Suddenly a fierce determination stormed through him, lifting up his heavy heart.

No, a life of scavenging would not do.

Cat squared his shoulders and set his jaw like a vice. And so it was decided. Cat declared north it would be. He took up the little figurine between his teeth and that last step out of the alley became his first toward watching the waves.

✧ three ✧
let sleeping dogs lie

The moment Cat resolved to leave, the setting of his youth was cast in a new light that made everything appear suddenly genial. Every landmark he passed now revived only pleasant recollections of his life there, almost as if his old haunts knew he was leaving and quickly donned their Sunday best to coax him into staying.

It was traveling down Sycamore Street, while all the town was asleep, that conjured the greatest nostalgia. For here on a neighbor's front lawn he had once experienced the first snowfall of the season.

As the snowflakes began spinning soundlessly down, Cat had imagined them to be white mice, paratrooping from some rodent planet. It was up to Cat to defend his homeland from this hostile takeover.

With all dispatch warranted by such an offense, Cat had set about pouncing on every snowflake that dared to land; melting these tiny terrorists beneath his warm paws.

It was a valiant assault Cat waged that day as he ran here and there defending his neighbor's home, reveling in the mere pleasure of motion.

Having considered his world saved, Cat remembered collapsing into a gratified exhaustion when he caught sight of two indoor cats. They sat pawing at the drifts that blew against their window. Cat recalled the little leap his stomach made when he realized the freedom that was his. It was simple memories such as this that acted as emotional trip wires, making him question his choice to leave. This wasn't the first time Cat met a causeless fear masquerading as an instinctual warning.

Ignoring his misgivings, Cat stayed his course. When he reached the crest of the hillside that framed the town, the same wooded hills that he had considered the limits of the world; Cat set Buddha down in a patch of wild grass and reminded him of his promise.

"So you were gonna tell me what 'put' me in that alley."

"Well, you said your freedom is what put you there, correct?" Buddha asked.

"It did. I thought I wanted that. But freedom didn't turn out to be all that great."

"Anything brought into being is less for the seeing," granted Buddha.

"The way I see it the world is just unfair," Cat sighed with a settled despair.

Buddha replied, "*Just* is the world that accommodates the beautiful and the 'unfair'."

"Then why don't I have a home? And why do all these undeserving cats I see have one?" Cat desired to know.

"The world takes you at your word," Buddha replied. "It appears you're the one who thinks you don't deserve one."

A black beetle glinted between the dry leaves. Cat began sporting with it, asking, "*My* word?" The upturned beetle worked madly to right himself.

"Your word is everything you think, feel and believe. Your home awaits you, but the world cannot bring it *to* you, the world can only bring it *through* you," Buddha said.

The beetle found his legs and scuttered away as Cat's resentments flared up, causing him to lose his temper *and* his prey.

"But I wouldn't choose this life for myself," Cat said darkly. "What makes you think I wanted to be a stray?"

"You desire a home and an owner but you also believe that the world is unfair, correct?"

"It is," Cat maintained.

"That's what your word amounts to; 'though I want a home, the world being unfair, I will not get one.' Do you see how the world would interpret your word?"

"I guess," Cat said suspiciously.

At this point, Buddha suggested they break off from their conversation and continue north through the hills. Never had Cat ventured beyond the reliable geography of his little town, so he turned and cast back a lingering look. As he did, there came a sharp poignancy, he realized this might well be goodbye. He dragged his eyes away.

Cat emerged from the wooded area and could see that signs of society began to dominate the horizon again. Industrial units lined narrow streets, deserted during these deep hours of the night.

And the yellow light slanting down from the sporadic streetlamps only rendered the desolation lonelier, the silence more profound. Despite its drear, Cat needed rest, so he began to seek any bit of shelter where he might sleep undetected. It was only after a long search that Cat crept into a darkened alley, finding a cardboard box that would serve his purpose. As he set Buddha down he heard a faint rustling and a sniff of inquiry.

Quickly, Cat raised his head and froze, holding his breath to listen. He had thought himself unnoticed but a deep voice cut through the evening air.

"This is my street!" it announced.

Cat dropped into a crouch at once, his tail thumping an anxious rhythm against the cardboard box. He knew this announcement welled from the throat of a dog.

"Oh, I didn't know," Cat said, wheeling around through the gloom, answering in the direction from which the dog's call seemed to come. "I couldn't see you."

"Everybody knows this is my street!" the dog said in a growly voice.

"I'm not from around here," Cat explained. "I was just hoping to rest for a couple of hours and be on my way, if that's all right."

Slowly, a shadowy form detached itself from an assemblage of rusted oil drums.

Out into the dusky moonlight came an enormous mutt. He was broad-chested, square-jawed and annoyed. He lumbered toward Cat to investigate. Cat's claws were ready for him. Looming over Cat, the dog inspected him with his chestnut eyes.

"Are you a stray?" the dog asked, rotten human food heavy on his breath.

"Unfortunately, I am," Cat admitted.

"What do you mean 'unfortunately'?" the mutt shot back. "Would you rather be somebody's slave?"

"Well no," Cat replied.

"That's all you are to a human; a slave," the dog informed him.

A chill of doubt rippled through Cat. Was he better off on his own? "I've never really been anybody's pet," he told him. "I don't know what to expect."

"I can tell you exactly what to expect. You can expect to be left alone for days on end with no food or water, and when the master returns and finds that you had to eat some of his food to survive, you can expect to have the hell beaten out of you. How does that sound?"

Here the dog smirked knowingly and sat heavily back on his hind legs. He appeared very well satisfied with himself for having painted so bleak a picture of what awaited Cat.

Clearly alarmed by what he was hearing, Cat began to pace back and forth like a caged tiger. "Is that true?" he asked.

"True as I'm standing here," the mutt said. Then, bending down to Cat's eye level, he thrust his large head toward him, displaying a welt that bore out his claims.

Cat shrank back and his eyes grew round. "What is that?" he asked.

"That's what you can expect!" said the dog.

"They all do that?" Cat asked, now visibly shaken.

"Every wicked one of them," the dog replied with a grim smile.

"Maybe I made a mistake," Cat said, eyeing the deserted streets.

"You did," the dog said. "You should have stayed in your own town."

Motioning toward Buddha, Cat said, "Well, my friend and I were trying to find a better place than that."

Searching the darkness beyond Cat, the dog put up his ears as if about to bark.

"What friend?" he asked quickly.

"Buddha," Cat answered as he lifted the little figurine around to show the dog.

The dog's ears dropped and his nostrils flared when he saw it. "That's a walnut, you fool!" he growled in his throat.

"Oh, no, he can talk," Cat said. "Say something to him Buddha."

"*You're* the nut!" Buddha said.

"Did you hear that?" Cat asked.

The mutt silently glared at Cat. He drew himself up to an appalling height and bared a trembling display of his side teeth. "Keep moving you lunatic!" the dog stormed. "And take your walnut with you!"

Cat's heart sank to his stomach and beat in his ears. He snatched up Buddha and retreated at the full speed his legs would permit. He was lit and concealed intermittently as he passed under the yellow streetlamps that lined the vacant road. When he got beyond the mutt's imagined scope of authority, he set Buddha down and stood gasping for breath, his sides heaving in and out.

"This is a mistake, Buddha," he said, shaking his head. "Let's go back, I don't want to be beaten."

"You won't be," Buddha replied calmly.

"But you don't know that, Buddha. You're not an animal. Owners beat their animals. You heard that dog."

"That dog was taking an image from his past and viewing each new day through it, thus never really seeing anything new at all."

Buddha continued. "Don't let all his fine bluster fool you, receiving any new experience requires an open heart, and an open heart requires a courage that dog does not possess."

It was close on two a.m. and Cat was eager to put the day behind him. He took up Buddha and prowled the streets for shelter. He walked alongside a corrugated iron fence topped by a coil of razor wire. Soon there came a small hole in the fence. Cat tilted his head to one side, shut his right eye and put his left to the hole.

The half-moon was overcast, yet by its light Cat could make out stacks of compressed cars in what appeared to be a wrecking yard. A few more steps revealed a length of the fence that was hung so crookedly one could slip through the opening and this he did.

Once inside Cat looked over the jungle of tormented fenders, bent axles and homeless engines that lay within the limits of the fence. He stood perfectly still trying to sense if he was alone. Convinced his only companions were the chatty crickets, he lightly hopped into a windowless sedan and settled onto a backseat of protruding foam and duct tape. He released a shuddering sigh.

In the distorting darkness, the contents of the scrap yard took on threatening shapes and he again questioned the wisdom of this journey.

"There is no need to dwell on the dog's predictions," Buddha said, answering Cat's unspoken thoughts. "He's obviously been hit in the head one too many times. I'd put another lump on his head if these arms could move."

Cat's attention was here diverted by a grating sound repeated in rapid succession.

"Click, Click, Click," it went. It was the nails of a dog against steel.

"Hey, over here, that one's broken!" Cat heard called out in his direction.

Looking out from his car, Cat saw a terrier, a stub where his tail used to be, leaning out the window of a wheel-less foreign coupe partway submerged into the dirt.

"Broken?" asked Cat.

"Get in this one!" the terrier yelled out with a slight lisp.

Soundlessly, Cat hopped to the ground, weaving through the mechanical debris and scraggly grass that separated the two cars.

"We're leaving as soon as our ship comes in," the terrier yapped as Cat approached. "This car is very valuable, it's the Gravy Train and the only one here that works, so if you want to leave you should ride with us," he told him.

Cat looked at the implanted coupe, which very well might have been the scrap yard's first inhabitant, and asked who the terrier was leaving with.

"My master," the terrier answered. "He's the night watchman and I'm the new guard dog since I ran away from the shelter."

The terrier began panting with the breeze that had just risen and, with his tireless stub wagging and his nose glistening, he shouted, "We're leaving!" But scarcely had he declared this when the breeze died.

"We didn't go very far that time," the terrier said as he settled onto the window frame. "But you'll want to join us because my master says we're going all the way once we find the rest of the parts for the Gravy Train," he added.

"All the way where?" asked Cat as he once again verified the absence of wheels on the car.

"Easy Street!" the terrier crowed. "When our ship comes in we're gonna ride the Gravy Train all the way to Easy Street!"

The breeze, as if on cue, blew again causing the dog to begin his nervous dance.

"See!" he said with his eyes wide, serious, as though his notions were now duly substantiated.

"They're getting crazier every minute!" Buddha said.

Cat saw a coming light and heard the sound of someone walking swiftly over the gritty dirt.

"Shut up, you, nothing's doing'!" a graveled voice called out from the darkness as the beam from a dying flashlight swept the area before them. Gradually, Cat could make out a shadow, then the shape of a man. A sunbaked man with grizzled hair and matching beard came into view. With a forward stoop to his shoulders and the sole of one shoe flapping, the night watchman shambled toward the car in which the terrier sat. Cat drew into the wheel well. From here he could keep his eye on all that passed before him without being discovered.

After lifting a bottle to his lips and draining its contents with one tilt of his head the man tossed it to the ground. It happened to land on a stone and broke with a loud noise. He took a wide stance to preserve his balance.

Positioning the flashlight on the hood of the car, he carefully compared a right side-view mirror he had found with the car's existing left mirror. Noticing a discrepancy he threw it down as sullenly as he could. A torrent of curses ended in a fit of bronchitic coughing that caused him to turn and spit on the ground repeatedly.

The breeze picked up, and the terrier, fringed feet braced on the car door, leaned out the window and barked into the wind.

"Shut yer yap," the watchman slurred as he pushed the dog back down onto the floorboards. The terrier went silent, his stumpy tail trying to curl between his legs.

The man leaned into the car, searching the cluttered ashtray for a cigarette. He held a twisted butt up close and squinted. Then, from his shirt pocket, he brought out a book of matches. A flare of yellow light illuminated his deeply etched face as he cupped his knotty hands against the wind. He puffed in vain.

He removed a tobacco flake from his tongue and pitched the spent match at the car. Cat drew farther inside the wheel well as the smoke twined its way up to his nose. He tensed his snout to prevent a sneeze.

The night watchman glowered at the stubborn car that would not so much as give him half a cigarette let alone carry him to a better life. He passed his fingers over the nicotine stained whiskers that had been with him for twenty years, then examined his watch. He turned his collar up for warmth and wandered back into the wreckage, mumbling into his beard and picking through the dead cars as he went.

Before too long the terrier reappeared, one ear turned up over his head. He scratched at a flea, happily anticipating his next excursion. The breeze rose and fooled the terrier once more.

While the dog, half in, half out of the coupe, was preoccupied with the traveling he wasn't in fact doing, Cat crept back to his car. Settling onto the cracked upholstery, Cat drew in his tail and wondered what exactly went on within the walls of the shelter the terrier spoke of.

He also wondered how long it would be before the terrier discovered the usefulness of the wheel and life beyond the scrap yard. As dogs go, this one seemed especially gullible. Yet as pitiful as the terrier's delusions were, the proud mutt remained just as immobilized.

No, to let another's beliefs about the world obscure your own would not do.

Not until late in the night did all become quiet. At last Cat grew drowsy and had just closed his eyes when a stupendous clash of metal sounded. He sat up and looked forth from the windowless car. He saw the night watchman rummaging through a nearby pile of automobile parts. Cat picked up Buddha and, jumping from his car, made for the boundary fence that marked the other end of the wrecking yard.

Just as Cat was collecting his paws together at the top of the fence, preparing to jump, he heard the terrier dance on the window frame. "Wait! Come back, we'll give you a ride!" he called out after him.

"Good luck and safe travels to you friend," Cat returned as he dropped softly onto the ground.

"Yeah, good luck with those travels friend!" Buddha added.

The scrap yard faded into the gloom of the evening as Cat continued his journey northward. He soon found himself entering a large wooded area. From this point on lay a doubtful world, fearful shadows beset his path and many foreign scents spoke of the new experiences that awaited him. The reaching arms of trees clawed at his flanks and the knotted underbrush gave way with sharp snaps. The wild growth that closed around Cat also teemed with sounds strange to his ears, the staccato tapping of a woodpecker, the guttural cry of a tree toad.

Nearby, a mockingbird crooned a stolen song and was answered in the distance by an even more obscure strain. In his uneasiness, Cat took it into his head that he was the subject of their conversation.

Cat managed to penetrate a great way into the woods and every trace of man's work was now far behind. He pushed through some dense brush and emerged upon an open glade with a single tree in its midst. The tree sat in a patch of pale moonlight, dead leaves strewn about its roots. Cat drew near.

Buddha asked if he would sit for a moment. Cat set Buddha down and tried to make a study of the outlying area, but the trees and thicket that encircled the clearing refused him even the slightest glimpse of what lay beyond.

"Can't we just keep moving?" Cat asked.

"Remember those things I was saying about your "word," Buddha asked.

"Yes, and?" asked Cat.

"Here's someone who can demonstrate that," answered Buddha.

Cat looked up into the tree under which he sat, but the clouded moon revealed not a single creature amongst the bare branches trembling skyward.

"Nobody's there," Cat said.

"The fig tree is there," said Buddha.

"I don't see any figs," Cat said, still looking up. "And I also don't see how you can compare my situation with a tree if that's what you're implying."

"You mean to say this tree is given its fruit every season but you have been left to anguish about the appearance of yours? You not only share the same majestic roots as this tree, but you've also been given the gift of creative freedom. This gift carries with it the responsibility of choice. You're free to choose the seed that you will plant, but then in strict accordance with the seed will the fruit in kind be produced. You are well aware of this law when applied to the fig seed and its tree, yet you are frustrated when happiness doesn't spring from your seeds of discontent." Buddha said.

Cat looked up at those leafless branches tick-ticking each other in the cold breath of winter. "What you're asking is hard in the face of things I've seen," he said.

"Face the things unseen," Buddha recommended. "To know peace you must first accept that all the seasons of your life have had their purpose. Now change your word and trust this iron law that governs all. Come spring all will see how the tree believed."

"The tree believed?" asked Cat.

"*Be-leaved,*" Buddha said. "Get it?

Cat made a little face. Yet, when he again looked up at the fig tree there was a hopefulness that was new in him.

And whether it was due to the progress the half moon had made or to the progress Cat himself had made, at the same moment, both Cat and the moon alighted on a tender bud, hardly there, on the slightest branch of all.

✧ four ✧
paths intersect

Cat awoke in the glade to a sunless day. With a swish of branches he exited the woods. He climbed to the rim of a solitary hill and looked out at what lay beyond. The first sight that presented itself was the largest loom of skyscrapers he had ever seen.

Never had Cat beheld such structures; reflective, angular, confidant. In the distance, great plumes of smoke billowed out from factory plants, uniting with the clouds and capping the sky with a leaden ceiling. Crowded freeways criss-crossed between the soaring buildings and columns of steam rose from grates in the street. Everything thrummed with progress and vitality.

"What is that place?" Cat asked.

"Just a city," Buddha answered.

"It looks dangerous," Cat said.

"Do you really know that?" Buddha asked. "You're sending your emotions out ahead of this moment, forcing them to fabricate what might be and distorting what *is*."

Buddha's words managed to calm Cat just enough for him to realize he was ravenous, and hunger being fear's master, the city now looked less like something to avoid and more like something that could fulfill his immediate need for food.

So down a long slope of grass and into the city the two of them went.

Cat's first impression upon entering the city, other than the noise and the crowds, was that wherever anyone happened to be they appeared in a great hurry to get somewhere else. It was an endless rush of man and machine. People spoke loudly into their phones and the many taxicabs and buses sounded their horns continually. The city on the whole struck Cat as a restless and agitated place.

"What's the matter with everybody here, it looks like there's a race going on," Cat commented.

"There *is* a race going on," Buddha replied. "A race to the future."

Cat had only traveled a short distance through the streets when, appearing out from a sewer pipe, a mouse scampered across his path, hardly sparing him a glance.

"Outta the way!" ordered the mouse, his voice resounding with unlikely depth.

Springing back a pace or two, Cat exclaimed, "Wow, even the mice are different here!"

"I'm sure he considers himself perfectly normal," Buddha commented.

Cat puzzled over the matter for a second; he didn't think mice could possess an attitude so disproportionate to their size. "I've never hesitated to go after a mouse before," he mused.

"Perhaps he can advise where one might find food," Buddha suggested.

To ask "food" where food is had never occurred to Cat. Tentatively, he called out to the mouse, "Excuse me, can you help us?"

The mouse turned and twitched his whiskers in the breeze. He gave Cat a beady stare, assessing his sanity. "Us?" the mouse asked.

"Yes," Cat replied, "where can I get leftovers?"

"Nothin' here leftover to get," the mouse informed him stiffly.

"No food?" Cat asked.

The mouse's face dropped with impatience. "You just get here?" he asked.

Cat furrowed his brow and feigned offense, hoping to create the impression that he was anything but a newcomer. But his antics betrayed him.

"I thought so," said the mouse. "Look, this place here's full of strays already and *they* barely eat. I can tell you right now you ain't gettin' no scraps before they do."

With that, the mouse scurried away as suddenly as he had appeared.

"I should have just eaten him," Cat said dryly.

"No, that was just another lesson for you," Buddha corrected, "One which was much more valuable than food."

"All I learned was there's no food in this place," he said irritably.

"Of course I only have ears of wood, but it sounded to me like you learned the mouse thinks there's no food here," Buddha replied.

"He should know, he lives here," Cat contended, still on edge.

"Like that mutt, he's telling you what is true in *his* world, not yours."

"This *is* his world," Cat said, indicating the urban surroundings with an impatient movement of his chin. "Not mine."

"I can tell you that there are as many worlds as there are pairs of eyes, and both are unlimited in how they may look," Buddha explained.

Cat stomped his paw as he rose to a standing position. "Well, I'm looking for some food and I don't see any," he said.

"I shouldn't wonder," Buddha responded. "No figs on the fig tree?"

"Nope!" Cat returned, continuing down the sidewalk. As he moped his way toward a crowded intersection, an image of the young fig bud he had seen came before his mind's eye. "Figs," he scoffed to himself. "Tuna's what I want!"

Then, quite on its own, the fig bud in Cat's mind began to quiver and expand. A fish wriggled itself out and dropped to the ground.

"Ha!" Cat exclaimed, stopping for a second. "What was that?"

"The world cannot bring it *to* you, the world can only bring it *through* you," Buddha reminded.

His mind still occupied, Cat stepped into the street failing to check if the traffic light was in his favor. It wasn't. He was sharply recalled from his thoughts by a great hooting of horns—cars from every direction came to a sudden halt, their brakes emitting a protesting screech. They stopped so short of him he could smell their burning rubber and feel the heat of their engines along his muzzle.

Cat willed his body skyward, achieving a height of which he had thought himself incapable, fairly flying to the sidewalk.

There was a confusion of angry voices and a general turning of heads. Then the cars continued with another screech through the intersection.

The traffic light changed, and the people who had been waiting on the corner began to cross. Cat exhaled in relief and, in the act, realized he was no longer holding Buddha in his mouth. He began to frantically search his immediate surroundings.

Looking up, he spotted a young boy with a mop of unruly blond hair midway through the intersection. With his wrist locked in his mother's grasp the boy reached down with his free hand to pick something up from the street.

It was Buddha.

Cat hastened back out into the intersection, but the boy had already slipped Buddha into his pocket. A paralyzing bolt of panic shot through Cat. He stood stunned in the very middle of the street.

Once again the traffic light changed and a cacophony of car horns now sent him flying to the opposing sidewalk. Skittish from the commotion he had caused, Cat could do little more than mechanically follow the boy and his mother.

Hundreds of people, all intent on their own affairs, were bustling their many ways down the sidewalk. Cat, threading a path through the maze of legs and iron-railed trees, saw the boy testing his pocket to make sure he still possessed his find.

Presently the boy and his mother rounded a corner, which took them for a moment out of Cat's sight.

Cat broke into a run, whipped around the corner and succeeded in catching a glimpse of the two just as they turned into a local market.

He trotted the short distance to the entrance and peered inside. A customer, coming from behind Cat, stepped on the rubber matt that triggered the automatic doors and walked past him. He could now see the boy pushing through the chrome turnstile, glancing behind as he followed his mother down an aisle. Their eyes met. Cat retreated back out to the sidewalk and there he waited.

Inside the market the boy and his mother worked at different speeds. The mother, inching her way along, checked the price of every item before dropping them into her cart, and the boy, all youthful impatience, skipped ahead, returned and skipped ahead again, all in an attempt to hurry his mother through. He even helped select oranges from a crooked pyramid and then loaded items two at a time onto the conveyor belt at the checkout.

An anxious half hour elapsed before the boy came running back out of the market ahead of his mother, stopping short when he saw Cat.

"He's still here!" he said, pointing.

"Don't touch it, I'm very allergic," his mother replied as she transferred the grocery bag from her right arm to her left and steered the boy by his shoulder. "I'm sure you are too," she added.

Cat reared back, then continued trailing them at a distance. As his mother dragged him along, the little boy periodically turned to observe Cat striding there behind them, his shoulders rolling rhythmically as he stalked the pair.

"Hey, he's following us!" the boy called out.

"Don't be silly," was all the mother replied, her careworn face glaring straight on.

Cat kept a steady vigil on the blond headed boy even as he was, now and then, swallowed from sight by the crowd. The boy and his mother eventually turned into the communal stairwell of a brick tenement. Cat paused on the stoop and looked up. The boy stole a wide-eyed glance over his shoulder. Cat began following them up the three flights of unlit stairs, noiselessly hopping two steps at a time till he arrived at their front door.

"Can I keep him, Mom?" the boy asked.

The mother, outraged that Cat had indeed followed them, pulled the boy inside and hindered Cat from going any further by securing the door against him.

"Certainly not!" was all Cat could hear as she slammed the door and threw a variety of bolts and chains in place.

And that concluded the matter. All fell silent. Only the hum of traffic from the street below made itself heard through the stairwell.

Cat sat dumbfounded. What now?

His shoulders, followed by the rest of his body, slumped over in defeat like a deflating balloon. Exhausted by the eventful afternoon, he dropped his head on his paws and tried to formulate a plan. But he slowly fell into a doze.

Drifting into a dream, Cat supposed himself a kitten again, back beyond all his troubles in the pet store. As the kittens were being given their breakfast, one customer, clearly agitated, stood pointing at Cat. "Don't give it *our* food!" she yelled.

In an effort to calm the disturbance the pet store's manager hurriedly escorted the woman out the front door; shutting it behind her with an angry bang.

Cat awoke with a start, a familiar scent filling his nostrils. He stirred to recognition of his surroundings, and as his eyes regained their focus, an object there on the doorstep slowly took shape. It was an opened tin of tuna.

❖

Cat had never been so thankful for a meal. The tuna filled him with a new resolve and vigor. Hoping to locate a window that might provide access to the boy, Cat tramped down the stairs, taking off two or three steps from the bottom. Glancing upward from the sidewalk, Cat saw, through the uncurtained windows, residents inside walking back and forth against the light. But none of the windows were within jumping range.

The only option that presented itself was to get to the roof by means of the neighboring tree, from which, the fire escapes that zig-zagged past the windows could be easily gained. Just so, Cat carried his plan into action.

Minutes later Cat found himself testing his weight against the metal grating of a plant-bestrewed fire escape, parts of which permitted a dizzying view all the way back down to the sidewalk. Cat quietly approached the nearest window.

The first apartment he peered into was inhabited by a woman, well-advanced in years, in a nightdress. Curled in her lap was a calico cat who lifted its head just as Cat moved away. A few more steps brought him to the next window where he saw the mother of the boy, towel turbaned on her head, the receiver from a wall telephone cradled between her shoulder and ear. She stood searching one cupboard after another in her kitchen. "I told you, I'm working Sunday, you have to take him. I'm sure you can handle both for *one* day," she said, accompanying her penultimate word with the slamming of a cupboard door.

But Cat found no sign of the boy and no Buddha.

Cat's exploits paid off when he lightly hopped onto the last fire escape and looked inside the window. His heart leapt. There was the boy, lying propped up on one elbow on an oval braided rug, absorbed in a game where he had Buddha conducting maneuvers with his collection of miniature soldiers.

Cat could see the boy. He could hear the boy. But as the boy was facing another direction, the boy could not see him. It was up to Cat to somehow attract his attention.

And so he mewed at the window, once, softly.

At the sound of it the boy whipped his head around quickly enough to displace the tangle of hair in his eyes. A surprised smile spread over his face.

"Hey! How did you get up here?" he gasped as he rose to his knees.

Dropping Buddha, he opened the window and lifted Cat inside.

"I *knew* we were gonna be friends!" he said as he set Cat down amongst the toy soldiers. "You can stay here with me. Only you'll have to hide if my mom comes in or else she'll make you leave." Then the boy picked Cat up again and raised him to eye level. Looking at him intently, he said, "I think I'm gonna name you Scout, okay?" The boy held him there for a minute more, searching Cat's eyes to see if the name met with his approval.

"Are you okay, Buddha?" Cat asked as the boy set him back down.

"That's Sergeant Buddha, if you don't mind. I've advanced in rank since you've seen me last."

"I see that," Cat said, admiring Buddha's impressive battalion.

The boy swept his plastic men aside with the back of his forearm, removing every remaining soldier so as to clear the floor entirely.

"I bet you'll like this," the boy said to Cat as he crawled halfway underneath his bed. He tossed his playthings left and right in a heated search. "Here it is," he exclaimed, reemerging with a device Cat could not guess the use of. He started manipulating the joystick that projected from its surface and Cat heard an electrical buzz emitting from a silver truck parked beneath the boy's study desk.

The truck began to move as if guided by some unseen hand. The boy's eyes brightened and he bit his lip as he showcased his most recent Christmas gift. The toy truck sped circles around Cat's paws as he calmly observed the possessed gadget. Having never been called into service as a child's playmate, Cat sat oblivious to the cue; making no effort to join in the chase.

A look of puzzlement came to the boy's face as the truck rolled to a stop.

"You don't like it?" he asked.

Cat sat looking at the boy.

"Hmm, what do cats like?" thought the wondering boy as he looked to the floor.

"Yarn?" he asked, having seen a crocheted depiction on his aunt's sweater.

Cat's tail went rat-a-tat on the rug in recognition of the boy's interest in him, though he had no idea what yarn might be.

"I don't think I have yarn but I have a ball," the boy said.

Again the boy submerged himself beneath his bed and rummaged for a moment or two, after which, he crawled slowly backward with a foam ball contracted in his fist.

"Here!"

He triumphantly presented the ball in his open palm as it gradually returned to its original shape. He then rolled it across the floor to Cat. It came to a stop at his forepaws and Cat looked down.

The boy nodded. "Roll it back," he encouraged. He waited a second, then retrieved the ball. Dropping onto all fours, the boy said, "Like this." He carefully nosed the ball over to demonstrate. This time when the ball came to a stop at his paws Cat dutifully nosed it back. The boy clapped his hands together and let out a celebratory "Yeah!" which he managed to laugh into many syllables.

"Cat, let us not miss our window of opportunity, shall we?" Buddha advised.

"Our what?" Cat asked, smiling raptly.

No sooner did he ask than the squeak of a door turning on its hinges was heard.

The boy's mother, slowly pushing the door open before her, appeared with an expression of alarm.

An expression equally matched by Cat and the boy.

"Tyler!" the mother yelled. She lunged towards Cat with both arms extended at their length. "I knew this would happen if you fed it!"

She made a grab at Cat's tail, managing to catch its tip when her head towel came unraveling before her eyes. Cat seized the moment, slipping through her grasp as she retied the towel. Instantly he whisked back out the window onto the fire escape.

Slamming the window shut, the mother pointed outside, warning, "If I find that mangy thing inside once more I'll have someone come and get rid of it for good!"

It was only her final two words that broke free from the clamor and floated out to the fire escape, yet Cat could sense that the "good" in "for good" wasn't good at all.

As the mother stalked out of the bedroom she pulled an inhaler from her pocket and brought it to her mouth. The boy ran to the window and pressed his face against the cold glass looking for Cat. He could see Cat trying to shrink from observation on a shadowy corner of the fire escape.

"Don't worry, Scout," said the boy in a near whisper, "you're gonna live here with me." Then he sat, chin in hand, drawing shapes on the misty windowpane.

Cat, unwilling to risk another run-in with the mother, crept from his place of concealment and jumped over to the furthermost fire escape on that level, which happened to be the one arrayed with the many potted plants and flowers.

The evening's traffic droned steadily, the occasional car horn sounding here and there. From this lofty vantage point, what appeared to be confusion below now revealed itself to be a grid of neatly laid out streets. All the city's inhabitants participating in a lawful rhythm.

Lying down, Cat cushioned his head on his paws, testing the possibility of sleep in such an exotic new setting. The sun melted into the horizon, the receding spread of rooftops and telephone wires flecked by the dying red disc. Uncountable city lights began to appear, winking like a sea of jewels. Somewhere in the distance a church bell counted out the hour and its dulcet tones were in perfect unison with the scene.

Under this calming influence Cat gave a raspy purr. It helped ease his frayed nerves.

"Well, hello little daredevil," quavered a voice from behind, breaking his reverie.

Cat quickly raised his head off his paws and, looking back over his shoulder, realized this fire escape belonged to the woman with the calico cat he had first seen earlier.

"Fear not, little one, I know you're probably hungry," she said as she began watering the night jasmine in her window-box.

Detecting sincerity in her soft Celtic brogue, Cat did not feel the need to engage in further fire-escape hopping this evening. She set her sprinkling can aside then disappeared back into her apartment. Cat heard the clatter of dishware. Next came the rattle of pellets—he craned his neck to look inside and saw her calico cat, who was also craning to look out. They both quickly withdrew.

The lady carefully backed out the swing-doors of the kitchen, ornate china rattling on a tea-tray. She placed the tray on the fire-escape. A saucer of milk, and heaped on a plate, cat food of the finest sort. Her gray hair was pulled neatly together in the back. A natural beauty still recalled in her matronly features.

Cat happily availed himself of the delicacies, though not without feeling guilty of deceit, for he feared his benefactress would realize by his appearance her neighborly hospitality went wasted on a stray.

"Come say hello to our guest, Emma," she said in a pleasant tone of command.

Then, returning inside, she lowered herself into a wide armchair, pulled a woolen shawl around her shoulders and picked up her reading.

Emma approached the fire escape with her pink nose quivering and her green eyes aglow. Her coat was a charming confusion of color and a tiny silver bell danced from her collar, providing a glittering musical accompaniment to her every move.

Cat did not wish to appear without manners so he offered her his saucer, which she generously refused. She stepped onto the fire escape and the two stood regarding each other for a moment. "Well, you know *my* name," Emma said, coming into a regal sitting posture. Then she curled her patchwork tail around her white paws and, nose high, waited for the return civility.

"Oh, yes, well, I don't exactly have a na...Scout! That's my name!" Cat said proudly.

"Why haven't I seen you before, Scout?" she inquired.

"This morning, I would have told you I was a stray," Cat told her. "But as of tonight I think my friend and I have found a home."

"I was a stray too before Mrs. Campbell took me in. Now I eat everyday and she reads to me at night."

"That sounds nice," Cat said.

"This is always open a little for air," she said, motioning toward the apartment window. "You and your friend could always visit. Mrs. Campbell loves cats."

Here Cat took his under lip into his mouth and dropped his head. "Well, my friend isn't exactly a cat," he said, looking on the ground.

"A dog?" she asked with a searching gaze.

Cat answered with a no that rose upward in a kind of singsong and hung in the air unfinished.

"Do tell then," she urged.

"I'm afraid to."

"Don't be afraid. I keep company even with the local pigeons, they bring me gossip from all over," she admitted.

"Okay but this is gonna sound really strange; my friend is a wooden figure I call Buddha who talks to me." Cat winced as he heard himself give utterance to his secret.

Then he lifted up his large eyes and ventured a momentary glance to register the effect of his confession. Emma appeared unfazed.

"That's not strange," she said in all earnestness as she returned to the preening of her chest. "Mrs. Campbell talks to a little figure named Saint Lucia."

"Really?" Cat asked, lifting his head.

"Yes, and Mrs. Campbell says she talks back," Emma said.

"That's a relief," Cat replied, "because I'm definitely hearing Buddha."

Cat became aware of a steady intoning coming from inside the apartment. Mrs. Campbell was reading to herself. Emma noticed his interest and suggested they go in to listen. Stepping politely through the window, Cat followed Emma to the corner of the room where sat Mrs. Campbell. Vermilion candles burnt dimly through their glass holders, spicing the air with cinnamon. Chamber music drifted from another room. The two cats lay attentively at Mrs. Campbell's feet listening to her read. Her pale blue eyes looking over to Cat each time her wrinkled hands turned a page.

As Cat sought to absorb something of Mrs. Campbell's kindly spirit, the tiny pendant that hung from a chain around her neck caught the light from one of the flickering candles.

"What's that 'T' she's wearing?" asked Cat.

After a moment's hesitation Emma smiled. "That's a *little trust*," she said with an intelligent nod of her head. For she had so often seen Mrs. Campbell clutching it, saying, "See Emma, all it takes is a little trust."

"Buddha says things like that too," Cat told her.

What Mrs. Campbell read quelled Cat's concerns and eased his anxiety. And though his weary mind failed to catch the exact words that flew overhead, the exact substance, having to do with never being alone, was apprehended by his heart.

Cat was in the middle of a luxurious yawn when the snap of the book closing gave him a start, bringing him to his feet. "Fear not, little one. You go back to sleep," Mrs. Campbell said as she lay aside her leather-bound volume. She reached out her hand. Cat came forward and raised his head to her palm. She began kneading the scruff of his neck then stopped when she recognized the absence of a collar.

"You can stay here with us little one," she said to him.

Cat brushed along her legs as a thank you. In doing so he left a patch of fur on her ankle stocking. She dabbed at her eyes with a balled tissue that obviously had been used many times before, then replaced it into the pocket of her nightdress.

"Goodnight my dears," she said, working herself out of her chair. She blew at the candles. The walls were her friends as she groped her way down the hall, for normally her legs required the assistance of a cane. She retired to her bedroom. Cat saw his fur make the trip with her and his guilt returned.

As Cat looked on, he could sense Emma's watchful eyes upon him. They held a silent question. To be here was to be Mrs. Campbell's loyal companion.

Cat was up to the challenge and eager to prove it, for she had won his respect. An unspoken agreement was taking place.

Unaccustomed to sleeping indoors, Cat bade Emma goodnight and returned to the fire escape. As he stepped outside he was met with a cool draft of night air. There he stretched his forepaws far out in front of him and began cleaning his whiskers in lazy comfort. What grand good fortune to happen upon this particular neighborhood Cat thought to himself. He never imagined so idyllic a scenario existed.

He rested his chin on his paws and hoped to enjoy the view awhile but his eyelids, being irresistibly heavy, allowed him only one more glance at the winking city lights.

As Cat began to drift off, a warning disrupted his peace. In spite of all the disappointments he had endured, he still retained a little seed of hope that he would find a home for himself. Now it felt as if that seed could take root here. He had let this happen before and it did not end well. But so kind were his hosts, and so secure was his lofty perch, that as Cat sunk into an abandon of possibility, a contented sigh escaped him.

A sigh that carried the warning away.

Farther than the farthest city light.

❖ five ❖

housebroken

"Scout! Hey, Scout! Come down!"

It was morning and the voice of the little boy was coming from the street below.

Cat was still hovering in the twilight between dream world and real when the boy's beckoning reached him. Bleary-eyed, Cat peered over the edge of Mrs. Campbell's fire escape and saw the boy's hopeful face looking upward. When the boy caught sight of Cat he gestured excitedly that he come down to join him.

Cat roused himself and arched his back high into the air. He stretched himself paw by paw. He tried to climb down the tree but his claws missed their hold. Suddenly the ground was rushing to meet him. By sheer effort of will Cat executed a midair readjustment and landed unhurt in a nearby cypress hedge.

Emerging from the shrubbery he came bounding down the sidewalk to meet the boy. Cat saw that he was engaged in a pick-up baseball game in the street with some six or seven other boys of similar age. The others were all decked in their colorful winter jackets and knit caps. But the boy played without a hat or jacket and his pants, clearly hand-me-down, were a size too big. He was forever hauling them up and one knee showed through a large hole.

Two boys and one girl deemed too young, too small and too female, respectively, served as spectators on the stoop.

"Hey, you guys, this is my cat, Scout!" the boy said, beaming.

My cat.

His teammates, still competing, came running over pushing at one another, their cheeks rosy from the cold and their breath rising in clouds. They doffed their knit caps and tossed their baseball mitts to the ground. Then they gathered round Cat, some leaning over, others on their knees. All assailed their teammate with a storm of questions.

"When'd you get 'im?" "Do ya get to keep him, Ty?" they asked on top of each other while Cat submitted to the boys over-petting.

Under normal circumstances, Cat could never endure this measure of attention; but strange alchemy it is when routine words alloy into a golden combination.

My cat

It was all Cat heard and his head was still reeling from the sweet intoxication of being so introduced. The boys returned to their game after a few cars passed by, yelling to each other in their high voices and quickly slipping back into a savage competition as only best friends can indulge in. All but Tyler forgot about Cat.

The fact that his novelty was so short-lived could not have mattered less to Cat.

He sat brimming with a sensation of pride that was as curious and new to him as it was pleasing.

At one point in the boys' game the ball rolled just beyond Tyler's reach, coming to a halt near Cat. Not one to let his lessons go unlearned, Cat stood up where he had sat and began nosing the ball back in the direction of the boy. Tyler collected up the ball, a raised arm displaying it in recognition of the feat. When his friends stood, mouths open and interest in Cat renewed, Cat had unknowingly reciprocated the feeling of pride that Tyler had aroused in him earlier.

As the sun disappeared behind the buildings, the shadows lengthened across the street. The boys, one by one, dropped out of the game, lifting their hands or chins by way of parting. Soon Cat and Tyler were all the company left.

To Cat's boundless delight, his patience was rewarded when Tyler came and joined him on the curb. Pulling out a stick of beef jerky from his back pocket, Tyler bit off a piece and held it out to Cat.

"Want some?" he offered.

Cat sniffed the offering then lifted it from his hand.

The boy caught his breath at the touch of Cat's rough tongue. He then stroked Cat's back as Cat pressed up against his hand. The boy confided in him many things that no one else in the world knew; the pain his parents' divorce had caused him, the boy who bullied him at school and the girl who didn't know he was alive. A wave of warmth spread through Cat, stealing up from his paws all the way to his whiskers, for never in his life had he been someone's confidant. He couldn't wait to share the news with Buddha.

Tyler bit off another piece of the jerky; his gaze directed a long way off. "When my mom sees what you can do with a baseball, she'll realize how special you are," he said nodding confidently.

As Cat sat gnawing on the jerky, a city bus, returning a group of commuters home from work, came to a stop nearby. The doors hissed open and among the first of the people that alighted from the bus was the boy's mother. When she saw Cat sitting on the curb, eating from her son's hand, her face hardened and she shouted, "Tyler, your allergies!"

Tyler stood with fading smile. Cat's chewing slowed as he began backing away.

She marched up with pursed lips and shook her paper bag at Cat to speed his departure.

"But Mom, you should have seen what he did with my baseball!" Tyler said, hot tears standing in his eyes, fingers spread wide in appeal.

"I don't care about the baseball, I told you to stay away from it," she said. "When we get home I'm confiscating that truck of yours."

"I didn't *do* anything!" Tyler complained.

"And if I find that Mrs. Campbell is taking in strays I'll be making a phone call, believe you me!" she added, wagging her finger in warning.

In the course of these remarks, Tyler shot a glance at Cat, who was by now on the opposite side of the street. Their eyes locked with a common longing.

The boy tried to push back the tears that damped his face, first with the heel of one hand, then with the other. Following his mother, he stomped home with untied shoes and a pout upon his lips.

Inwardly, however, he felt more rebellious than ever.

An hour thereafter, Cat, yearning to know his fate, eavesdropped unseen on the fire escape as the boy and his mother sat at a folding card table, bent over plates of fish sticks and green beans. Their voices were pitched low at first, but Cat listened with his eyes and could tell by their gestures they were debating. The quarrel grew more and more heated and as their voices rose in key the boy was heard to say, "But you said I could have a pet!"

"I said a goldfish!" his mother corrected as she brought her open hand down on the table, causing the silverware to crash together. She collected up her son's knife and fork and began cutting his green beans. "Here, you can't just eat the fish sticks," she said.

After his dinner, Tyler, contrary to his usual custom, volunteered to go to bed early, smuggling a tin of tuna past his mother. Once safely in his room, he peeled open the tin and placed it on the windowsill. "Here Scout," he called out quietly into the night.

He listened, turning his head to hear better. There was no answering patter of paws. Cat was still lingering on the fire escape, watching the mother touch her lips with the edge of her napkin then scrape back her chair. Cat saw her open the door to the pantry, counting the remaining tins of tuna. She gave a weary sigh and dropped her shoulders. Then she pulled the inhaler from her pocket and gave it a shake. Making her way to the telephone, she lifted the receiver. Cat drew near the window so her voice would be the more distinct.

"Hello Mrs. Campbell, I just wanted to tell you that I know you're housing a stray and I'm calling animal control." She hung up quickly, paused a second, then lifted the receiver again and punched three digits.

"May I please have the number for animal control?" Cat heard her say.

As the lagging hours wore on, Tyler sat hugging his knees in bed, banked up with pillows, watching his window. He knuckled his eyes, trying to stay awake with all his young might. But towards ten o'clock with still no sign of Cat, the long day of baseball finally caught up with him.

In her apartment, Mrs. Campbell was hurriedly packing an overnight bag.

"Don't worry girl, they'll never take you away from me," she said to Emma as she placed her in a carrier. Then she rushed out the door, leaving a trail of clothes and overturning a chair in her haste.

Cat, all the while, kept to the darkness and shadows of the rooftop, putting a safe distance between him and the mother until all went quiet. The night was well spent before Cat ventured from his hiding-place. Stealing noiselessly down onto the fire escape, Cat found Tyler's offering on the windowsill and there took his evening supper.

"Well, look what the human dragged in!" was the abrupt remark that made Cat's head jerk up mid-chew, his cheeks full of tuna. It was Buddha, and Cat looked at him as though he were seeing him for the first time.

"Oh, hey. I didn't think the window would still be open," he said as he resumed chewing the now tasteless food, his mouth turned down at the corners.

"It is, and we should use it," Buddha advised.

Cat turned his head to one side, narrowing his eyes at Buddha. "*Use* it?" he repeated in a high tone like one surprised. "You're not saying we should *leave*, are you?"

"I am," Buddha answered.

"Oh, no, I'm staying! And don't try talking me out of it." Cat said.

"Do you think that entirely wise?" Buddha asked.

"En-tirely!" Cat returned, disappointment sharpening his tongue.

"Didn't you say you wanted to find a home for yourself?" Buddha reminded.

Cat sashayed into the bedroom and lounged elaborately on the floor, his belly distended with food. "What would you call this?" he rebutted with a toss of his head. "Isn't this a home?"

"Not yours," Buddha admonished gently.

"The boy has already named me, and I've *never* eaten this well. What else could I want?" Cat pressed his case after a temperamental pause.

"May I point out that the boy's mother has no intention of letting you stay?"

"You just wanna go 'cause I'm the one getting all the attention now!" Cat said, his face growing warm.

"Cat, it is not your destiny to cower on a fire escape for fear of being discovered. It's not your destiny to disrupt people's lives by staying where you don't belong. And most important, it's not your destiny to stop your discovery *here.*"

Cat sat up resolutely. "I don't have a *destiny,* Buddha. I'm lucky I found this. Do you want us to end up back in some alley? We could stay with Mrs. Campbell and Emma if we can't stay here. Aren't these the things you said I could have?" he asked heatedly.

"You have succeeded in attaining food for yourself, you've succeeded in attaining a greater sense of self-esteem, and you succeeded in becoming aware that not all humans are unkind to animals, but I am here to tell you, you're postponing your happiness and fulfillment out of fear."

"And *you're* meeting Mrs. Campbell and Emma!" Cat retorted as he collected Buddha up.

Cat vaulted over each of the three fire escapes with fluid agility. The opening of Mrs. Campbell's window seemed unusually narrow but still Cat was able to slink through. Keeping his chin and belly to the ground, Cat crept into the apartment, moving just inches at a time. Considering the lateness of the hour, he proceeded with a silent tour of inspection.

"Emma, you awake?" he whispered.

The living room, lit only by the moonbeams that were looking in, appeared to be in a state of disarray. Cat stood for the second or two that it took his eyes to become accustomed to the dark, then continued on.

He thought he saw something stirring in the room and, tracing it to its source, realized it was his own exaggerated shadow repeating his movements against the wall.

Abruptly the refrigerator came alive with a rattle, then settled into a mechanical purr. Bygone pets watched him trespass from framed photographs adorning the walls. He recognized a charcoal sketch of Emma.

"Emma?" he tried again.

Cat crept down the hall and peeked inside the bedroom. A bedside clock ticked in the darkness, showing one a.m., but there was neither sight nor scent of Emma or Mrs. Campbell.

"Go back into the living room," Buddha told Cat.

Cat passed lightly into the living room.

"Bring me over to that figurine there," Buddha said.

Cat drew closer to the bureau that displayed the icon of Saint Lucia as its centerpiece. Her hands were pressed together, palm to palm, in an attitude of prayer.

Her face fractured with time. Two tiny dots of black paint were placed there to represent illumined eyes. Close by stood supplicant pillar candles.

"Emma and Mrs. Campbell have left," Buddha told Cat.

"Is she talking to you?" Cat asked.

"She is," Buddha answered.

Buddha was silent for a moment. "The boy's mother has already set plans in motion to have you removed from here," he said.

As Cat listened, an image of Tyler's mother on the telephone came clearly to his mind. He recalled what she had said.

"By morning men will be looking for you," Buddha said.

Cat remembered the warning he received on the fire escape. He now knew his little seed of hope was not meant to take root here.

No, even this would not do.

"We have to leave tonight," Buddha told him.

Cat felt himself letting go of something he'd been holding onto. Something he knew wasn't rightfully his. He slipped back out the window. Then hopped weakly across the fire escapes, one, then two, then paused on the third, which led to Tyler's bedroom before entering.

Inside, all was darkness, but for a blue moon nightlight near the floor, the boy's foam ball lay within its lunar glow. The breeze from the window fluttered the pages of a comic book, his silver truck conspicuously absent.

Tyler slept between the folds of his blankets. Cat placed Buddha on the oval rug then crept soundless as a shadow so as not to wake the boy.

He stole close, taking occasion to breathe in the boy's familiar scent; a scent he would remember long afterwards. He addressed Buddha without turning his head. "You know that he's gonna be okay?"

"That I do," was Buddha's simple reply.

"Okay...let's go," Cat said tonelessly. He picked Buddha up, bringing him back onto the fire escape.

Gazing out over the many crooked housetops and city lights, Cat then turned and looked upon the boy who made him love the world again. He lay in the innocence of sleep, one hand under his cheek, a tangle of hair over his eyes.

As Cat sat watching, the bedroom door slowly began to open. He hid himself and saw the boy's mother come softly into the room with his silver truck. She placed it beneath his study desk.

Leaning over her son, she turned one ear close to his mouth, listening. She smoothed back his hair and pressed a kiss to his forehead. The boy stirred, the bedsprings creaking as he turned over with a groan. She wrapped the blankets more snugly around him, then stood and allowed a smile to take shape. In this private moment she appeared small, alone. Cat chided himself now for thinking poorly of her, for not understanding.

As she was leaving the room the breeze lifted the curtains. She turned and noticed that the window sat open. Cat dropped from sight as she came over and quietly closed it, not noticing him crouching there. She drew the curtains across the world outside.

It was time.

In the morning the boy would call from his window, down in the street he would call, then he would go to sleep that night knowing Cat was gone.

With his heart caught in his throat, Cat could only manage to whisper, *"Tyler and Scout...Tyler and Scout."*

⋄ six ⋄

a new master

By daybreak the streets of the city were already thick with traffic. Cat looked up at the slits of cold sky that showed between the high buildings. His mind had not lost itself in the roar of the traffic for more than a minute when a thin and rough-coated cat, who had been lurking nearby, breezed up to him.

"Hello, my name is Jerry," he said, sounding like a nametag. "Looks like you could use a little assistance!"

Cat eyed him quietly for a moment. His smile was eerily human and his tail serpentined about as if it had a life of its own. Cat stammered out a word or two about being lost.

"I can help you with that!" Jerry responded.

A shade of doubt passed across Cat's face, as this seemed suspiciously accommodating. Jerry saw his apprehension and adjusted his efforts.

"Look, I'm not trying to sell you anything, all I'm saying is we all feel a bit lost from time to time. But I know someone who can help you with that," he said, standing closer than necessary, staring at Cat with fixed, unseeing eyes.

Before Cat could make the least reply Jerry draped his tail around Cat's back and guided him down the sidewalk. "Come," he said.

Then he sent out a peculiar yowl, which produced another cat who was one-eyed and swaybacked. The newcomer appeared by Cat's side and immediately dropped into step with them. The two gaunt cats nodded significantly to each other from over Cat's head.

"Where ya off to?" the new cat asked.

"Oh, hey Steve, this lucky cat is going to meet Victor!" Jerry answered.

"Oh, wow, you *are* lucky!" Steve replied, his attention directed to a point somewhere above Cat's head, then somewhere about his breast, but never to his eye.

"Who's Victor?" Cat asked, then saw in the glance they interchanged this was someone a city cat would have already known of.

"Victor's the guy who can help you not feel so lost anymore," Jerry said. "Once upon a time I too felt lost. Victor helped me with that. What about you Steve, Victor ever help you?"

Steve played his part, rolling his remaining eye and saying, "He's the only guy in this world who has!"

The trio was now traveling empty streets on the outskirts of the city. The two strays that flanked Cat leaned against his shoulders to steer him around various corners.

Cat saw rows of condemned houses set back from the road. After a few blocks the houses gave way to factories from which hung signs advising the curious to keep out.

Soon they were chugging him along railway tracks where no trains ran anymore.

Cat worried his own plan was in danger of derailment.

"Where are we going?" Cat asked, his voice shaky from the jolty surface. "I should probably be getting back now."

"So you're saying every little thing in your life is working perfectly?" the cat named Steve asked, hoping to find some disappointment he could use.

"Well, no, but I think my friend Buddha can help me with those things."

"Oh, that's dangerous thinking, my friend," Jerry said. "But don't worry, Victor can fix that too."

When finally they reached a derelict gas station, Jerry began pawing at its iron roll-up garage door. He hung his head and waited for permission to enter. The delay Jerry and Steve now had to endure seemed to make them uneasy. Addressing no one in particular, Jerry remarked, "Boy, this weather, I'll tell ya, is spring ever gonna get here?"

He gave a forced laugh, as did Steve. Cat responded with a small laugh to go with theirs.

"Not trying to sell something my foot!" Buddha said. "Let's get away from these characters."

Cat positioned Buddha and himself out of earshot and argued that in contrast to the others they had come across on the street, these cats, despite their unconventional ways, were honestly trying to help.

Jerry and Steve were huddled close and appeared to be quietly quarreling.

"The only difference between honest people and dishonest people is honest people are more discerning in what they lie about," Buddha remarked.

Two feline guards from inside the garage peered out from under the roll-up door, looked Cat up and down, then withdrew. Jerry slithered under, followed by one-eyed Steve. Then Jerry turned and said to Cat: "Come in."

And in went Cat.

Hardly had Cat entered the gas station when he became inexplicably restless— the air was thick with damp decay and charged with a peculiar energy. Inside were many other cats in groups of two, threes and fours. It was obvious that outsiders were a rarity because Cat quickly became the subject of interest.

Ragged pigeons fluttered noisily about the rafters. Cobwebs veiled the walls and ceiling. Old tires filled every corner and along the dusty floor lay rust-eaten gas cans and the tracks of rats that never made it to their destinations.

The gas station in its entirety was a monument to another age and its contents were more worn by time than by use. Somebody had washed their hands of the venture long ago. Cat noticed that the living accommodations appeared to be communal and the cats in the gas station busily toiled away at one task or another with the expressionless eyes of goats. And though these cats were of all ages and breeds, they were somehow strangely alike. But just how, Cat could not have said. Not yet.

"Wait here," Jerry said to Cat and Steve as he ducked into an adjoining room that had once been the office. After a few minutes he poked his head back out and motioned them inside. The stench emanating from within assaulted Cat's nostrils from where he stood. He breathed through his mouth as he entered and the odor was soon accounted for.

Once inside, Cat found himself in the midst of a semicircle of gaunt cats who were congregated around one enormously bloated beast of a cat—Victor himself.

And in Cat's wide experience of unsavory characters, this creature stood unrivaled for repugnance. His tang was almost suffocatingly powerful.

It appeared a ceremony of sorts was taking place. A hearty, well-groomed cat stood before Victor. After a moment of thought Victor leaned over and rasped a single word to his attendant. The attendant then announced; "You shall henceforth be known by your Victorian name: 'Craig.'"

The newly christened cat gasped in delight as he was ushered from the room.

"You look so different now!" someone said to him as he passed.

Jerry approached with his tail carried low and performed a bow. He remained in this posture till Victor directed him to rise by certain signals of his forepaw.

"Victor, this lost soul needs your help," Jerry said, referring to Cat.

The imposing Victor leaned over and croaked some instructions to one of his attendants. "You may petition Victor now," the attendant announced.

Noticing that every pair of eyes, some twenty altogether, were fixed on him, Cat looked at Victor and then at Jerry and then at Victor and then at Jerry again. From the awkward silence that followed, Cat sensed that he was expected to say something. "Who, me?" he asked.

Jerry turned toward Cat and silently formed the words: "Yes you."

Cat found it a challenge to collect his thoughts under their combined gaze, but he managed to begin, "Well, I've never been to this city before and I'm just trying to find a place to settle but…"

Before Cat could conclude, another of Victor's attendants cut him short, proclaiming, "Victor has agreed to help you."

At this Cat's whole body was set to hope.

"First you must recognize Victor as the only truth and free yourself of all Non-Victorian possessions," the attendant let it be known.

Looking puzzled, Cat stated, "But I don't have any possessions."

Victor quietly conferred with the attendant. It was related that Buddha was the Non-Victorian possession Cat was to foreswear.

When Cat informed them he considered Buddha a person, not a possession, and would not consider surrendering his hold on him, a collective gasp rose up from the assembly. Jerry moved forward amidst a cascade of murmurs.

"May I request council?" he asked.

Victor motioned for silence and approved Jerry's request with a nod.

His aide then declared, "Victor grants a three-minute council to member Jerry."

Jerry ushered Cat back into the main body of the garage, stopping on a square of light that skewed in dustily through the only unbroken window.

"Do you understand what you're doing?" he asked in a surprising change of tone.

"I can't give him Buddha," Cat said.

Jerry, recovering his self-possession, said, "Look, you don't get what's going on here because you're new, but let me ask you a question. What do you think is gonna make you happy?"

"Me and Buddha are just looking for some kind of home," Cat answered.

Jerry inspected him shrewdly and asked, "And you want that because you think it'll make you happy, right?"

"Something like that, I guess," Cat conceded.

"I hate to be the one to break it to you, but you ain't gonna be happy there or anywhere else unless you first achieve Victory," Jerry said.

All the time Cat was thus indoctrinated, various group members in the garage were making a great show of camaraderie between themselves. Others stole glances at Cat from the corners of their eyes, and were quick to go expressionless or offer smiles when noticed.

"Victory?" asked Cat.

"Yes, when you recognize Victor as the only truth you achieve Victory over the nine lives...you know you only have nine lives, right?" Jerry asked with the self-assurance of one who knowingly held the upper hand.

"Nine lives?" Cat repeated.

"Yep, nine little lives and then it's over. Unless of course you're interested in what Victor has to say. After my ninth life I'm gonna transition into a human

70

just like Victor," he said smiling. Then he turned sober, adding, "And by the way, I can tell you're definitely on your ninth right now."

"Victor's a human?" Cat asked, glancing back at the office.

"Looks like a cat to me," Buddha commented.

"Yes, and if you transition into a human you won't have to rely on somebody else, you can just make your own home," Jerry said.

"I didn't know that was possible," Cat said.

"Don't feel bad about not knowing. Most cats don't. But you're lucky enough to be around the one guy who can make that happen," Jerry said.

"Victor?" Cat asked.

"Yup. But you're gonna have to commit to the process if you wanna see results."

Cat sat exploring what felt like new dimensions in his mind. Ideas began to rearrange themselves. As Cat sat breathing in the influence of the charged air, suddenly it hit him. The reason his life had spiraled downward was simply due to the fact that he had lacked the truth. Most cats did. It was clear now if he wanted to claim that truth as his own he would have to clamp down on it with a steely commitment. He imagined transitioning into a human and making his own home.

"How long does it take?" Cat asked.

"That all depends on you my friend," Jerry told him.

"When can I start?" Cat asked.

"Right now!"

Having perceived the desired change in Cat, Jerry followed up his advantage by guiding him back inside the office and there announcing, "Fellow Victorians, this is no lost soul you're looking at...he has *recognized*!"

The room erupted with repeated shouts of "Ultimate Victory!!"

A circling dance developed around Cat and the remainder of the evening was given over to celebration. Individually they came forward and congratulated him enthusiastically, his praises on all their tongues. One of their number, a wheat-colored Siamese, told Cat he should take pride in seeing the wisdom of joining their group. It took a special sort to recognize.

Cat never had a party thrown in his honor before, and this was not without its effect on him, for he experienced the tantalizing lure of fellowship for the first time.

Amidst all the festivity, a youthful Snowshoe named Nancy came and laid her tail across Cat's back. A bewitching scent stirred his senses.

"Come, I'll show you your sleeping quarters," she purred.

As he was being escorted back out into the garage, all the revelry made Cat feel so free of his cares and concerns, he failed to notice he had been made free of his Non-Victorian possession as well.

❖

"Get up! Hey, get up!"

It was Nancy trying to jostle Cat awake. Before he opened his eyes, Cat felt the room suddenly come to life as the scrabble of many claws rushed back and forth along the cement floor. He heard someone shouting abuses in the background. He tried to locate himself. Then it all came crowding back on him; this was the neglected gas station where all the cats possessed human names.

"What's happening?" Cat asked, blinking the sleep from his eyes.

"Morning worship!" Nancy told him.

"Morning worship?" Cat repeated. "Where's Buddha?"

"Let's get going we're late," she said.

"Who took Buddha?" he asked again.

She gave Cat a chill smile. As impatient as she was, she was duty-bound to indulge new members.

"That thing you were carrying around was a false idol, you're about to meet the real thing," she replied.

She hurried Cat into the office where all of Victor's members were already assembled in neat rows before Victor. Guards stood watch from every corner.

More than a few heads turned to look and judge the latecomers. Cat took his place between Nancy and another member with dilated eyes. "Welcome friend, I'm Stanley," he said to Cat.

Sitting upright, Victor was held in balance by the numerous folds of fat that lined his torso. His forequarters hung slack on opposite sides and his breath wheezed as it came. He cleared his throat and began his sermon.

" I, Victor, was once like you, a lowly animal. Bound to the whims and whimsies of the human world."

"Master," the room chanted.

"I now walk through the human world as their equal. A human. You will see my human form when you are ready."

"Master," they chanted again.

Stanley sat mesmerized by Victor, his mouth slightly parted, his eyes unblinking.

Cat squinted at Victor, trying to make out his humanness.

Victor continued, "You too will transition just as I did if you are willing to relinquish all non-Victorian possessions, adopt a human name and never, ever diverge from the doctrine."

"Master!"

"Do you see Victor's human form?" Cat asked Stanley.

"Oh no, I'm not ready yet. But I hope to be someday," Stanley answered.

Cat could already feel disillusionment settling in. He resolved to rescue Buddha.

But now, because heads were beginning to turn, he knew that would require something dramatic. He worked his brain for a plan. "Stanley," he pressed, "did you have any Non-Victorian possessions when you first came here?"

"Just my collar and name tag," Stanley answered.

The idea that Stanley had not been a stray before he'd arrived here was indeed a strange one to Cat—one that made his mind race with many questions. But unfortunately, the circumstances allowed Cat to ask only one.

"And where did that collar and name tag end up?" he asked lightly.

Cat's question was not met with an immediate response. Its mutinous undertones were clear to Stanley and he knew full well the punishment that awaited one involved in an unsanctioned withdrawal.

"Stanley, I don't think you're gonna turn into a human, you should come with me," Cat said.

Stanley gave Cat a sympathetic look, as though stress were causing him to speak nonsensically. "But you haven't even been awarded your Victorian name yet," Stanley replied.

"I don't need a Victorian name, I need to know where they took Buddha," Cat said to him.

Stanley realized his words would be of no avail upon Cat. He relented and told him he would find Buddha in Victor's private playroom: the little bathroom at the opposite corner of the garage.

In the same second that Cat turned to make one final appeal at luring him away, he saw a burst of movement reflected in Stanley's dilated eyes. From behind, the guards, who had heard everything they said, were lunging tooth and claw at the two of them. For the briefest of moments, Cat and Stanley's eyes truly met. And in that instant, Cat saw that Stanley no longer belonged to himself. That he would never leave the group.

One of the group members pitched himself upon Cat and the two of them rolled out into the main body of the garage, locked in battle. Claws lashed wildly and teeth flashed. The combatants crashed into a stack of tires with force enough to stun and separate them momentarily.

Now.

Cat took his cue, and with all haste slipped inside the little bathroom. There he put his paws to the task of feverishly paddling through a trove of confiscated belongings until Buddha surfaced. It was none too soon, for Cat had scarcely retrieved Buddha before a stocky Siberian appeared in the doorway, a spark of sanctioned violence flashing in his eyes. Howls and hisses coming from the next room told Cat the group members had now fallen savagely upon Stanley.

"Victor's playroom!" the Siberian in the doorway told the others.

Onto the bathroom sink Cat leapt, and from there dove out a jagged window that broke the skin along his belly. With Buddha firmly in his mouth, Cat hit the street running at a furious speed, droplets of blood trickling from his smarting wound.

He was only half a block away when he heard the sound of falling glass. For a second he thought it might be the remnants of his own hasty exit but now rapidly approaching footfalls suggested he was being pursued.

A quick glance over his shoulder confirmed that one of the members was making straight for him, not twenty lengths behind and cutting down the distance that separated them with long lean strides. Cat made a hard turn down a side street and the member was still in attendance, settling the question whether or not he was the hunted. With that dreadful confirmation and all the force of his fear behind him, a bolt of adrenaline lent him wings and Cat easily scaled the high wooden fence that sealed off the alley he had turned into. Cat heard the member do the same with distressing swiftness.

The landscape that confronted Cat on the opposite side of the fence offered nothing in the way of an obstacle course. Nothing to crawl under, leap over, or otherwise confuse or slow down his assailer. Here lay a stretch of open road that pitted one cat's naked speed against the other. The glaring lack of escape possibilities sapped much of Cat's energy and he heard, in the acceleration of paw steps behind, what was dispiriting for him was a source of encouragement for his pursuer.

In the course of the hot race, the member slipped and sprawled on an oil stain. But then it was up and away in an instant. Cat had no idea what he was doing now beyond delaying the inevitable. Panting heavily and losing his lead, Cat felt his journey had come to a crisis and his hope could not have been more completely gutted when a low growl sounded from behind. Was this reinforcements sent by Victor or had they attracted a dog into the chase?

As they ran, a beam of light began spreading onto the pavement before them, and with it the growl grew louder. Judging from the vibrations underfoot it could be guessed that it was a large truck traveling toward them. It was indeed a big rig, behind schedule on a cross-country haul.

Cat's mind began exploring the ways in which this development might prove serviceable to his cause.

His first thought was to somehow leap onto some part of the vehicle and be whisked away to safety. But this turned out to be impossible as the truck came thundering by; its tires alone were more than three times Cat's size, making the truck far too big to cope with. Cat followed in its immediate wake and seemed to be altogether at his pursuer's mercy. Just as the member was on the point of overtaking him, Cat charged ahead then crossed the front of the massive eighteen-wheeler, cutting it so close there was no possibility for his opponent to do the same.

Cat had rightly guessed that his pursuer had not the time to follow him around the front, but in a desperate attempt to cut him off, the member darted underneath the freight trailer in front of the rear axle. The roar of the diesel engine drowned all lesser noise and prevented Cat from hearing a sickening thud twice repeated. The driver spared no more than an irritated glance into his side-view mirror.

Cat was still sprinting frantically as the truck motored away into the distance ahead, and hearing only his own paw steps, he glanced behind. He saw his pursuer turned aside from its purpose, staggering piteously in a different direction now. Holding one hind leg off the ground, it wavered on three legs away from a fresh smear of blood.

The modest curb the member endeavored to climb still proved too great a height and when next Cat looked behind he saw the member lay down in the gutter and move no more.

Cat slowed his retreat, then paused a minute before deciding it was safe to investigate. He padded back towards the motionless figure at a very cautious pace.

Standing over the body he slowly turned it onto its back and beheld the face of Nancy, blood bespattered and crooked with pain. Her mouth sat opening and closing automatically, emitting broken sounds. She looked up at Cat as though he were a long way removed from her. She drew a long breath. She blinked one last time.

Then her eyes filmed over and she lay frozen in her final agony. Now it was she who seemed far away. As Cat looked down at her lifeless body, illuminated in part by the single streetlamp, he felt a stab of remorse. If only he could make her again what she had been one minute before.

Who was responsible for this wasted life? Could he really lay the blame at Victor's door when it was her own unquestioned obedience and willingness to exclusively think another's thoughts that had fatally misguided her?

Already, buzzing flies began to gather around her eyes. Cat tried shooing them away but the swarm simply rose up then settled back in place.

Knowing it was only a question of minutes before Nancy would be looked for, Cat backed away then turned to go. He assumed the group members would bury her remains near the gas station but in fact Nancy would be reported as "dead weight" in accordance with Victor's policy and would putrefy in the gutter until removed by the city.

Away, with a scurry, Cat ran across the miles not looking back. All was quiet except the puffing of his breath and the pattering of his paws on the cold streets. Never had Cat moved so swiftly over the earth as he did on this day.

Away, with a scurry, past the smoking factory plants and the people who planned to impound him.

Away, and still away Cat went. Beyond the condemned houses and the cats who sought to control him. The last city building was an hour behind when his legs refused to carry him farther.

Cat now found himself in a desert unmarked by foot, wheel or paw. He set Buddha down and collapsed in relief and exhaustion. When finally he recovered his breath, he broke the silence that reigned in this remote area.

"Buddha, why didn't you warn me about those cats? You must have known what they were up to—why didn't you say something?"

Buddha responded, "If you'll remember Cat, I did, but when your mind closes, your ears and eyes are imprisoned by your own conviction."

"I'm just glad to be outta there," Cat said at length. Yet even as he spoke, his thoughts were with Stanley and what he might suffer for his share in the escape. This weighed heavily on him as he nursed the wound on his belly. The scar that would eternalize his memory of the group.

Pausing from his work, Cat turned to Buddha, "Why wouldn't he leave?" he asked.

"Those unready to face the truth merely pounce on its shadow," said Buddha.

Turning to Buddha, Cat asked, "What do you mean?"

"Because Stanley has never directly experienced the truth of his own being, he's attributed that truth to Victor. Victor has further persuaded Stanley that there are forces working against him and his teachings are Stanley's only hope of overcoming them."

After a moment of meditative reflection, a new spark of understanding ignited within Cat. No, to live one's life in strict accordance to another's rule would not do.

Cat gave a long exhale, then narrowed his eyes against the breeze that puffed past his face and ruffled his fur.

He was free again.

⟡ seven ⟡
the desert well

Cat gazed out into the darkness just as a vein of lightning split the air and briefly illuminated the entire desert.

Racked with fever, Cat's body was still fighting the wound it received from the broken glass. And to that same end, Buddha had Cat eat a few sprigs of horsetail grass to help heal his wound and build his strength.

Cat felt safe being away from the outskirts of the city where Victor ruled but the open desert made him feel slightly vulnerable. So he felt compelled to hold watch with both eye and ear. Worn with watching, Cat soon dozed off and his fever bloomed into a flamboyant dream. In it Cat found himself wandering the desert with a young deer possessed of a great and mysterious power.

Cat was expected to protect the deer from its one vulnerability: the roaming hyena of the desert, who tried with all their might to distract Cat.

In the dream Cat would stay vigilant until the hyena overwhelmed him and the little fawn would fall helpless. Just as readily, the hyenas would entice Cat away from the fawn with a potent catnip. Cat would emerge from his euphoric stupor only to find the fawn being dragged away by the laughing hyena.

The hyenas were blindly unrelenting in their mortal efforts, and were in mid-attack when Cat awoke with a sudden jerk. His fever broke with the morning. He urgently sniffed the air. He stood, scanning the desert from every quarter of the compass. On all sides lay endless copper sand. The occasional rock formation and sagebrush the only options for the shade-seeking wayfarers during the seasons of heat. Roving shadows from the clouds passed over the land and far in the distance stood a great mountain range.

Sky, desert, a cat with a small figurine. That was all.

Relieved, Cat let out his held-breath.

"Sleep well?" Buddha asked cheerily.

Cat told Buddha of his dream, asking if hyenas existed in the region.

"Oh yes, plenty," Buddha answered.

"Plenty?" Cat repeated. "Then why are we going this way?"

Buddha's assurance that Cat would not leave this world by way of a hyena attack did little in the way of restoring his composure.

So Buddha swore, by virtue of his mastery over time and distance, it was within his knowledge that Cat would emerge from the desert intact. Cat consented.

For though he was uncomfortable with the prospect of crossing a desert, Cat realized, as they had already committed so much to this route, retreat no longer stood as an option.

"Those mountains might hold some promise," Buddha said.

Cat indicated he agreed by moving toward them.

Wandering so far through such unchanging emptiness gave Cat's mind opportunity to wander too. But unlike the desert, his mind was far from empty. He worried he might be going the wrong way, he worried the hyenas would show up, and he worried his dinner would not. His worries multiplied with each mile they crossed. Cat also developed a slight limp, and as his spirits sank so did his pace.

"Keep going," Buddha encouraged.

So Cat did, and did not stop.

With nothing to relieve his discomfort, time became heavy. Cat looked up to see a pair of hawks, high against the roof of the sky, whistling and circling.

"Those hawks…" Cat said lifelessly.

"They'll keep their distance, as long as they know you're strong," Buddha reassured him.

"But I'm not strong," Cat moaned.

"It's up to you to show them you are," Buddha replied.

Cat's head hung low and his lips caught on his dry teeth. For even the winter sun was strong enough to evoke his thirst. Up ahead something shimmered.

"I see something," Cat said. Then he cocked his head asking, "Could it be water? Is that a well?"

With heart beating and mind anxious, Cat broke into a clumsy run. As he neared it, the alluring vision resolved itself into a petrified tree, bleached by the sun.

Its twisted branches sloped downward and from its base flowed not water but giant rats, for here lay the mouth of their nest. He dropped Buddha on the sand and stared, disbelieving.

"There's no water," he whispered.

"If you place the mind *before* the eye all becomes a mirage," said Buddha.

Cat was overcome. He felt the desert had become a metaphor for his life with all its evaporating promise.

Giving full vent to his frustrations, Cat shouted, "I knew this a mistake. Nothing I do is right! I must be meant to die of thirst out here. And I might as well because nobody's gonna miss me anyway."

Then he slumped over, utterly dejected.

"And so the hyena have come," Buddha said.

Cat spun abruptly around. "Where?" he asked.

"In your restless mind," Buddha explained. "In your dream the hyenas represented your self doubt. I applaud your symbolism. Nice choice, Cat."

"So I was only imagining them," Cat said, relaxing a little.

"No, they were real," Buddha said more seriously. "'Nothing I do works' is a hyena, 'I must be meant to die of thirst out here' is a hyena, and 'nobody will miss me anyway' is a hyena."

Cat turned and looked back. The sand was broken by a long chain of his paw prints. He turned to Buddha. "What about the fawn?" he asked.

"The fawn is your mind at peace," Buddha answered. "Which you will only find when you stay present."

Cat contemplated the twisted tree that, in his delirium, he took be a well. The rats now all having returned to their nest.

Buddha continued, "The hyena will try and drag you away from the present in any way they can because they cannot exist there. They will use fear, they will use fantasy, but the one thing they can never afford to do is leave you alone; because it's your attention that gives them life."

Cat saw that sagebrush grew more plentiful in the distance ahead. He observed the mountain range, whose bold outline stood black against the violet sky. Nightfall wasn't far off now.

"Dreaming of the hyenas was a sign of your willingness to let go of fear," Buddha told him. "By recognizing the hyenas only exist in your mind they become powerless."

Cat sat very still taking in the idea. A strange peace descended upon him.

A solitary breeze whipped past like a messenger. The horizon grew hazy. The sand dulled and turned russet. Turbulent clouds came rushing on, darkening as they advanced. Scattered drops quickly dotted and discolored the sand. A rumbling in the distance arose as towering misty columns began moving across the desert.

Cat closed his eyes and turned his face to the drifting rain.

⋄ eight ⋄
ascension

Night came, and with it an increase of rainfall. The moon broke free from a congregation of clouds. Cat walked in the moonlit rain and kept his eyes to the mountain.

The barren country behind gave way to scenes of plenty as Cat and Buddha continued toward the mountain range and the majestic forest that surrounded it.

And the more the vegetation grew the more nourishment Cat found. Here and there were tufts of wet grass crawling with beetles and locusts. Each passing tree rose taller than the one that came before and from the many edibles he found along the way Cat began to regain his strength.

By the time they entered the deep shade of the forest, ranks of stately oaks and pine grew in groves, and the canopy of branches and foliage intercepted most of the rain.

Buddha suggested they take advantage of the harbor the trees offered and pass the night there. So as the wind rushed through the top of a leafy live oak, Cat nestled into its gnarled roots. Eventually, he fell asleep.

At daybreak a band of crows perched in the oak's branches began cawing that the dawn had arrived. Finch and thrush hopped about the musky leaves gathering twigs for their nests. Cat stretched and splayed his forepaws. He licked the dust off his nose and gathered Buddha in his teeth, then set out into the raw morning. Where he went he hardly knew. The pathless forest was dense and Cat lost his sense of direction.

At the end of an hour, when Cat thought the next turn would bring them beyond the margin of the forest, there, some two or three yards ahead, stood the live oak that had been their bed. Cat gave an exasperated sigh, "I think we've made a complete circle."

Buddha thought the top of the pine tree they were standing under might give them a better sense of where they were. Cat agreed this was a good idea so he scaled the tree. But the view from the topmost branches, which bobbed with his weight, only revealed the mountain range.

"I guess there's only one way to know what's on the other side," Buddha said.

Cat did not want to hear it but knew he was right.

"If you come to a mountain, climb it," Buddha said.

Cat swallowed nervously and nodded his readiness. Then he descended the tree and they journeyed in the direction of the mountain. As they finally neared, Cat stopped and tried to scan the mountain from base to peak, but its Alpine grandeur rose far into the sky and its summit was beset by dense storm clouds.

"Where does it end?" Cat asked.

"I guess we'll find out," Buddha replied.

The many rocks that occupied the foot of the mountain pointed in every direction and getting from one to the next required that Cat pick each step carefully. Their glassy surfaces also added much to the risk. At first he slipped off the rocks as much as he stayed on them. Ultimately, though it cost him several small cuts, Cat managed to negotiate the craggy terrain. Further up, the rocks proved more manageable, rising in a series of equal steps. Cat was making excellent progress when he picked up a strange scent.

"What folly is this?" a voice called out from behind.

Cat turned a surprised look and saw a donkey. He had stumpy peg legs and eyes that moved independently of each other. His awkward appearance was made all the more comical by the wildly serious expression he wore.

"What do you mean?" asked Cat.

"Surely to goodness you know of the mountain lions?" the donkey snorted.

"Mountain lions?" Cat asked.

"You'll not encounter a more wicked lot in all your life. And this is not limited to the lions, this mountain is filled with every kind of depravity you care to name. But make no mistake, judgment will rain down and the earth will swallow this place whole. Save yourself and turn back now!" said the donkey.

Looking faint at the probability he himself was conjuring up, the donkey then glanced uneasily at the mountain. As he did so, there came a thunderclap, causing him to bray loudly and hobble back down the rocks with many backward glances.

"Definitely an ass," Buddha remarked.

This sent Cat back in his thoughts to his encounter with the mutt from the alley.

The drizzle now turned into a thick rain. And when there was no rock to support Cat, the wet soil would sink under his weight; his tracks behind quickly filling with water. This slowed his pace and made the trek that much more difficult.

Pausing for breath, Cat turned to check on the view, but the lay of the land appeared no different than from the top of the pine tree. He glanced behind at the faint footpath, trying to gauge his progress. Clumps of small trees studded the hillside, obscuring his view. As he turned to resume his climb, something shot through the scrub. He moved towards it and found there a gray-brown rabbit. His upright ears trembling against the wet leaves.

"You ain't eatin' me, so keep movin'!" the rabbit said when he saw that Cat had spotted him there.

Cat felt a rush of relief. "I'm not going to eat you," he told him. "You can come out if you want."

The rabbit loped out and sat up on his haunches. Dabbing at the air with his nose, he said, "You're a cat. What's a cat doing here?"

"I'm trying to see what's on the other side," Cat told him as he set Buddha down.

"You better watch out, *you* might get eaten," the rabbit warned. "There're mountain lions here, you know."

"I've heard," said Cat.

He told Cat of the strong winds reported near the summit and of all the other dread consequences he'd surely encounter should he venture higher. Then the rabbit hopped away and disappeared down his burrow.

As Cat watched, his mind wandered back to the city mouse who had tried to discourage him. How odd that things repeated themselves he mused.

"He's telling you what's true in his world not yours," Buddha said.

Collecting Buddha back up, Cat set his jaw with a new firmness of purpose and was off again. Often it happened that he would see snakes winding in and out through the grass, their scales wet and reflective from rain.

Also, every here and there, a stone or two would come toppling down from above. Cat froze with each one, wondering if the fulfillment of the donkey's predictions had come. Further up still, he had to balance himself along narrow ledges that plummeted steeply down the face of the mountain. He was ascending one such ledge when, from behind, the clip-clop of hooves signaled the approach of a little regiment of mountain goats clambering up the same ridge.

"Outta the way!" one of them bleated at him.

Cat quickened his pace, but still the nimble-footed goats gained ground. In an instant they were crowding past him. One butt him from behind. Cat lost his footing, but he eased his hindquarters, little at a time, back onto the ledge. He put on some speed and pulled ahead of the pack. Knowing the goats would only catch up again, Cat leaped over to the first recess of level ground he came to, hoping they would pass on. But the goats turned into the recess as well.

"I almost fell off!" Cat complained to the goats as they filed in one by one out of the rain and pressed around him. A bearded male who appeared to be the spokesman for the group leaned forward and squinted at Cat, first with one eye, then the other.

"Are you one of their cubs?" he asked in a shrill and reedy voice.

"One of whose cubs?" Cat asked, edging back.

"Why, the mountain lions, of course," he answered impatiently.

Cat informed them that he was not a mountain lion and in fact had never even seen one before. The goats explained that the social order on the mountain had become hierarchical ever since the mountain lions arrived. No animal could explore the upper regions without their consent. "Think they can impose whatever regulations they like and we're all just supposed to follow along. Must be an awful lot of food up there, bunch of bureaucats, if you ask me," he groused.

"You'll be their dinner unless you join," the smallest among them announced importantly.

"Join?" Cat asked as he searched the assembled faces for meaning.

"Goats Against Bureaucats," the one who had butted Cat proclaimed with a sparkle of expectation in his eyes, as if Cat might recognize the moniker.

"Never heard of it," Buddha said.

For a second Cat felt a flash of fear and wondered if he indeed needed the protection the goats claimed only they could provide. But then he recalled feeling this way once before. An image of Nancy's body lying in the street came to his mind's eye.

No, to band together in fear, in a gas station or on a mountainside, would not do.

"I'll take my chances alone," Cat replied as he pushed through the group and bolted back up the slope, not bothering to look behind to see what the goats thought about him passing on membership.

Their discordant bleating gradually tapered off as Cat toiled up the mountainside. A few minutes more and it died away altogether, leaving him alone with the sound of the rain.

At last the trail developed into a well-defined path, widening as it went. Cat thrust himself upward as best he could.

Later, his legs resisted his efforts as he edged himself out onto a shelf of rock that jutted out over the forest. He craned his neck and strained his eyes through the rain. But though he looked this way and that, still just an ocean of billowing treetops stretched away and away, too far for his eye to measure.

At these stony heights the oxygen was getting thin. Cat was beginning to see faces swarming in the rocks. His muscles were pleading for rest. When he happened upon a large cavern, in which he could hear the echo of dripping water, he decided to take shelter there. He entered the cave through the overhang of vine and tree roots, on which hung a delicate fur of frost, his plan to stay only long enough to rally his strength.

But when Cat felt the strangely warm stone floor under his bones he was overpowered by exhaustion and soon fell asleep. He found himself returned to a desert scene where, in the way of dreams, he and the fawn had now exchanged roles. Never had Cat known the degree of serenity he felt there in the care of the fawn. Cat looked up into its glowing eyes.

"The fear is gone," Cat told him, amazed.

The fawn, as if to verify this, leaned over so that the movement of its breath touched Cat's forehead. The sensation became increasingly vivid until reality reasserted itself and Cat realized he was being sniffed at by a large gang of mountain lions.

✧ nine ✧
heaven and earth

"He lives among men."

One of the mountain lions was relaying to his brethren the message that Cat's scent bore. He dragged his whiskers up and down the length of Cat's body, seeking further information. Knowing the odds were against him in both fight and flight, Cat held as still as death. Indeed, fear had taken the strength from his muscles, forcing this third option.

"Keep still Cat," Buddha told him.

"Give an account of yourself," a male who looked to be the eldest among the mountain lions commanded. Cat's eyes darted from one lion to the next as their powerful bodies steamed in the cold.

"I'm lost and trying to find a home," he made haste to answer.

"Then why come here?" the mountain lion countered.

Recalling past results of disclosing his relationship with Buddha, Cat was not willing to risk the whole truth with the cougars. He felt it wisest to give into a bit of innocent fiction.

"My instinct told me the mountaintop could help give me direction," he said carefully, then he grit his teeth and waited.

The mountain lions, who were huddled over Cat, raised up their heads all together and nods of consent were exchanged. The answer seemed to satisfy them. They broke ranks, opening a means of passage between them so Cat could continue his ascent.

There was something ceremonial in their ways and Cat dismissed the predatory nature attributed to them by the goats and other animals he had chanced upon.

Like some mythic scene, Cat cut a path midmost through the pride, a voice inside telling him these cats had played a part in his ancestry. For an instant he was no longer a cat but a mountain lion among them.

Urged to new efforts by the cougars' favor, Cat made his way out from the mouth of the cave, braving the hard weather. Tucking his chin against the wet wind, which was being propelled directly into his face now, Cat went his way up, up, up the jagged steeps.

And as the degree of incline would increase, so did the degree of temperature decrease. Drops of rain now had a trick of only bouncing once or twice before turning into arctic pearls.

Fierce gusts whirled about Cat's ears and sounded like the laughing hyena. He paused.

"They only exist in your mind," Buddha reminded.

Cat exhaled and resumed his climb.

Rain began ringing hard against the rocks. Cat looked up. He saw ghostly figures slowing curling all around him. He was in the clouds now.

He tried to distinguish the landscape below, but so thick was the mist; even his own tail was quite hidden in the fog.

Obeying his heart alone, Cat pressed upward filled with a strange expectancy, though for what, exactly, he could not have said. He only knew he must now go where his journey had not yet taken him. He must.

And as Cat rose higher and higher and higher still, so, too, did his hopes. He felt a great daring wake to life within him. He defied the weather and incline of the mountain as if he had known no travel or fatigue. An ancient instinct powering his limbs. With one mighty effort, Cat took two blind steps into the teeth of the storm. Immediately his paws flew out from under him and he began tumbling uncontrollably. The rain, bucketing down, took away his sight and the wind, calling high and strong, blotting out his hearing.

Earth then sky, over and again. And then Cat knew no more.

❖

Cat's eyelids flickered. It was some time before he could bear the light. As his vision adjusted, he found himself in a world of sun, snow and sky. It seemed to him that perhaps by some miracle he had gained the summit; and so in fact he had. Here then was the final plateau above the clouds, below which nothing was to be seen. Cat sat up, coat hanging sodden and chin dripping. He began drinking in crystalline air few animals would ever taste. His breath hung in white clouds before him.

Beneath him, the ground was sheeted with a slight covering of snow that was newly fallen.

The sun shone brilliantly and the snowscape shared in its brightness so that he felt balanced within an eternity of light. Cat shivered as the sun began sending pinpricks of warmth throughout his body and drying his weather-beaten fur into clumps. He shook himself vigorously, scattering beads of ice water into the air.

"Are we at the top?" Cat asked.

"We are," Buddha answered.

"I must have fallen asleep."

"Yes, and for quite a while," Buddha told him.

Lonely winds whistled past, sounding like the notes from a wood flute. Cat looked down and realized, due to the cloudbank, they had ascended beyond the point whereby he could tell what was on the other side. "Now we're too high," he said.

Just then a spectral figure began flickering into view. Cat gave a sharp intake of breath. He stood poised for instant flight.

"Wait, am I still sleeping?" Cat asked. "Are you seeing that too?"

Cat blinked hard but this did nothing to dispel the vision.

"So that's what those mountain lions were all about," Buddha said to himself.

Cat stared in speechless wonder, his eyes as round as teacups, his ears laid back, flat on his head. "What is it?" he asked.

"It's an ancestor of theirs," Buddha replied.

In a twinkling the figure acquired clarity and now that Cat had full opportunity to observe he could see that it was an aged mountain lion. Never had Cat seen eyes so patient.

"I don't think we belong up here," Cat said as he made a motion to turn around.

"Wait," said Buddha. "He's saying something."

"Saying what?"

"He said you've done well," Buddha answered.

"That can't be right," Cat said. "Tell him we haven't found a home. Tell him I'm still a stray."

Buddha was silent for a moment. "He said stray is something you do, not something you are," he relayed.

The sun was just starting its westerly decline and the crisp air currents were suddenly rising, creating thin rows of snow dunes along the mountaintop and dashing Cat's matted fur about.

"Ask him which direction we need to go. Ask him if we're ever gonna find a home for ourselves," Cat cried above the howling wind.

"He said always home, never alone," Buddha replied.

Here the mountain lion moved to the northern edge of the grand cliffs, leaving not a single indentation in the snow to mark his passage, there he looked over. He flickered and, in a twinkling, was gone.

Cat walked over to the edge too and saw, through a break in the clouds, the patterned lights of a town far below.

⋄ **ten** ⋄

metamorphosis

Down Cat looked at the lights of the little town. He could feel it in his bones that he was standing on the threshold of a new life. Somehow he felt happy and sad both at once. An influx of memories passed before him. He reflected on the story he was leaving behind. About the cat he used to be. And about his first meeting with Buddha. How long ago all that seemed now.

"We've come a long way," Cat mused.

"We can stop here for the night," Buddha said.

Cat found a spot that sheltered him from the wind. He licked the tired pads of his forepaws, contemplating what lay ahead. Then he lay down exhausted and glad for sleep.

Cat blinked his eyes in the low morning sunlight. He raised his nose to gather in the scent. A clear revelation of the town now lay open before him like an unfolded map. It was not the urban sprawl of the city, but a sleepy cove town nestled at the foot of the mountain. All the houses clung to the hillside, the one overlooking the other, sweeping down to a sheltered bay on which glints of sunshine madly danced, now on one part, now on another.

Cat and Buddha began their descent and it was an altogether different affair from their ascent. It seemed the storm had exhausted itself and shafts of light from the sun were now beaming through rifts in the clouds. The fog that had obscured the mountain began to break apart, and the birds of the forest ventured out of their nests and filled the air with such a variety of notes, Cat could scarcely tell one call from another.

"No goats or donkeys on this side," Cat commented.

"Can't say I miss them," Buddha replied.

They reached the basin and finally entered the town. Cat was thankful for its smooth, tarred roads and temperate climate.

As they began traveling through the picturesque community he became concerned with the picture he presented; what with his tattered coat and Buddha's baffling presence in his mouth, he worried he might be seen as suspicious. But after a young boy proved he was willing to venture a petting, Cat's trifling concern was swallowed up by the more pressing matter of finding a safe place to spend the night.

Soon Cat found that food began to dominate his mind. Following his nose, and the urging of his empty belly, Cat was led to an alley lined with waste-bins where he decided he would sample the local fare.

Just as he began rocking his haunches side to side, preparing to launch himself into a bin, a slinky tom, carrying a crumpled food wrapper that masked his face, emerged from inside, out onto the rim. Cat let out a screech of surprise that shocked the tom into a desperate dance to secure his footing, which ended in a backward plunge into the bin. Cat sprang to the perimeter and apologized for the scare.

As the tom drew himself out from the garbage, the embarrassment on his face showed that the bin had not only reclaimed its wrapper, but got the cat's dignity in the bargain as well.

"I didn't see you there," the tom said as he lazily scratched behind one ear with his back paw. His coat, bearing the marks of many a scrap, was as inky-black as it could possibly be, with the exception of a small patch on his chin as white as paper.

The Tom hoisted himself back onto the rim and he and Cat nimbly leaped down from the bin to the pavement below.

As an introductory overture, and to free the tom from his embarrassment, Cat explained that the little statuette he carried with him was his traveling companion Buddha. "We're looking for a place to stay," he told him.

The tom introduced himself as Ming. "Maybe you could stay where I stay," he suggested.

"Where is that?" Cat asked.

"I'll show you," Ming said.

And so Ming and Cat pattered on, the one behind the other, through a manicured park, atop a brick wall, between the crooked gravestones of a hillside churchyard, until finally they came to an old apartment that Ming said was his home.

The two of them leapt onto a balcony overflowing with discarded furniture, among which, numerous drowsing cats were making their homes. Only one of the residents bothered opening one eye, regarding Ming and his guest.

They stepped through the sliding glass door. The only two signs of activity in the dirty apartment were the enormous flies that went lancing in and out of columns of sunlight, never seeming to land, and the wiggling of cat ears when they did.

"Easy to see why he prefers waste-bins," Buddha said.

An elderly woman emerged from the kitchen. "Is that your owner?" Cat asked.

"That's her," said Ming.

That's when she noticed Cat. She rushed back into the kitchen and returned with a raised broom in her hand. "Oh no you don't," she said waving the broom at Cat. "We've got ourselves a full house already. Go mooch off of someone else!"

"Thank you for trying Ming!" Cat said as he fled from the woman. He headed out through the balcony and jumped to the street.

"Don't worry Cat, that place was not for us," Buddha said as Cat trotted briskly down the sidewalk.

"That's fine with me," Cat said. "I did that already."

No, the life he once led would not do.

Cat and Buddha approached an intersection filled with pedestrians waiting to cross. The red traffic light that hung over the street brought to Cat's mind images of a great commotion, and to his ears, the echo of angry voices.

Cat took this as a sign. "I should probably wait here," he said.

From the crowd, he felt someone's attention trained on him. "I don't think it belongs to anybody; no collar," Cat heard.

On twisting himself round, Cat saw a woman with bobbed blond hair and blue eyes set widely apart.

"Hello you," she said kneeling down next to him. She gave Cat an affectionate stroke of his back. "I think it's a boy," she said to the friend that was with her as Cat's nose inspected her fragrant hand.

"Hey, whatcha got there?" she asked, referring to the little figurine Cat was holding in his mouth. Cat took a fresh grip on Buddha and two noncompliant steps backward.

"Oh, no, that's okay. That's yours, I know," she told him.

Looking up at her friend she made a painful grimace as she pointed out Cat's knobby spine. "I should bring him back to the store and feed him," she said. Then she turned back toward him. Cat watched her closely as she stroked him. There was a gentle concern written in her eyes that subdued his habitual impulse to flee.

The light was no longer red now, and as she stood up and dusted her hands one against the other, something metallic glinted from around her neck that commanded Cat's attention. He repositioned himself as he followed her across the busy intersection, struggling to decipher the source of the light.

Noticing his interest, she turned down toward him as they walked and raised one eyebrow a fraction. "You hungry?" she asked.

That's when Cat realized the "light" was the sun's, reflecting off a little 'T' necklace that she wore. Cat thought of Mrs. Campbell and took this as another sign.

He continued to follow the woman along the brief but lively strip known as St. Cloud Court. Aimless afternoon browsers shuffling in and out of the shops mixed with lunch hour employees lagging back to their jobs.

Two blocks later, she stopped to bid her friend goodbye. The two women attempted a hug, but their efforts were prevented by the many shopping bags that hung from their arms. They both laughed and mimed a kiss as they parted. Her friend stepped into the street and placed her bags inside the trunk of her unwashed white convertible.

"Yes Tia, I know I need to get it washed," she said.

"Good lord, how long has it been?" Tia asked, laughing.

"Yeah, well *you* need to give your new cat over there a bath if you're gonna go adopting him," her friend winked as she rounded the hood and opened the door.

"I'll just be feeding him thank you," Tia called out.

Her friend smirked then turned the ignition. "Sure you are!" she said, pulling the sunglasses that were perched atop her head down against the afternoon glare. Then she merged into the flow of traffic and waved.

Tia studied Cat a moment then said, "Okay, come on then."

Cat trailed along as she led him further down the street, periodically turning to verify his presence. Some minutes later she stopped before a small flower shop, letting an elderly couple stroll past before she announced to Cat, "Here we are."

Cat warily eyed the giant yellow sunflowers that stared out alien-like from the front window.

"They won't eat you," Tia said with a laugh as she turned her key in the bolt-lock.

The wood-framed glass door resisted for a second before the clang of the brass bell announced its opening. She entered and, with a gesture, indicated that Cat follow her.

The perfume of the flowers held Cat at the doorway a moment.

While flipping around the CLOSED sign, Tia glanced down. "Come in," she urged.

Cat did not obey without a searching glance into the shop first. Tia walked to the back, lifting the flap of the counter and depositing her bags behind. Cat entered softly after her, taking in the burst of color from the great array of flowers.

She came back around and, kneeling down, squeaked open her Styrofoam container, which held her leftovers, and placed it before Cat.

Cat made an examination of its contents, gave it one lick, then dug in hungrily.

"Oh, it's a buddha," Cat heard. Looking up, he saw Tia turning Buddha over in her hand.

"Don't worry, I'll just clean him up for you," she said, taking Buddha beyond the door that warned: EMPLOYEES ONLY, into the backroom where a paper-bestrewn desk faced a kitchenette.

Drowsy from the heavy meal, Cat snoozed while Tia washed Buddha in the sink.

Before too long the bell on the door gave notice of the arrival of a customer. A young man in mechanic coveralls shyly admitted he wanted to surprise his wife on their first anniversary.

Tia made up an arrangement of red and white roses. After putting the finishing touches on the ribbon she stood back to get the effect.

She assured him of a hero's welcome as he counted his crumpled dollars into her hand. As he exited he held the door for a mother and daughter who were hoping to find something to liven up the girl's first apartment. They looked casually about at the flowers then went on to examine every polished leaf of the potted plants.

And so it went for the remainder of the day. By closing time Tia had forgotten all about Buddha who lay hidden between coffee mugs in the sink.

"Time to go home," she said to Cat as she turned off the lights and held the door for him. But Cat stood his ground within the limits of the store.

"You want to stay?" she asked, surprised.

In answer, Cat turned and strolled away from her.

Looking downward, Tia placed one hand into the small of her back and a finger across her lips. "Okay, why not…you can stay the night," she said with a shrug of her shoulder.

Producing a plastic bottle of water from her purse, she poured its contents into the lid of the Styrofoam container should Cat get thirsty.

"Goodnight," she called out.

The bell rang for the last time of the day as she closed then locked the glass door.

After she left Cat returned to the entrance. The flower shop now received its only light from the streetlamps outside which came filtering in through the blinds and fell in lines across the checkerboard floor.

Cat lay down, tucking his paws under him. He drummed the tile with his tail, then yawned, showing his pink tongue.

He glanced back at the EMPLOYEES ONLY sign on the door that separated him from Buddha. He then turned and observed the OPEN sign that now hung facing him on the back of the front door.

Cat had quite enough signs for one day so he curled beneath the watchful eyes of the alien sunflowers and promptly fell asleep in the flower shop on St. Cloud Court.

✧ eleven ✧

spring

By the time Tia arrived at 9 o'clock the next morning, Cat had already seen the storefronts surrounding the flower shop come to life. Shades were raised, doors were opened, window displays redressed for the coming spring.

"Good morning," Tia said in a musical voice, the jingle of the brass bell accompanying her as she entered. She half expected Cat to be out the door at his first chance, but to her surprise he just calmly eyed the cat food and water bowl that she carried in with her.

Tia gave Cat his breakfast, flipped the OPEN sign on the door and began freshening up the flower arrangements. After his meal, Cat curled on the floor by the counter. One eye opening with each new sound in case the EMPLOYEES ONLY door should be opened.

During the midday hours a lull between shop bells left Cat and Tia alone with the hum of a rotating desk fan and the faint classical strains from the radio atop the floral cooler. Tia sat immersed in a crossword puzzle, periodically blowing the surface of her coffee. Cat dozed by her feet.

The jingle of the bell announced the arrival of someone.

Cat blinked his eyes and saw a woman in well-worn jeans. She had fiery red hair and carried an armful of flowers. "What is this?" she asked.

Tia looked up from her crossword puzzle. "Maggie!" she said with a guilty smile.

"Did you get another cat?"

"He followed me to the shop yesterday," she explained. "So I thought I'd let him stay the night?"

"Of course you did!" Maggie laughed as she tucked a loose strand of hair behind one ear and bent to Cat. "We just have to be careful, azaleas are coming in," she said stroking Cat's head. "No tags?"

"Nope. But he did have something with him." Tia got up and went into the back room. She returned with Buddha in hand. "He was carrying this in his mouth."

Upon seeing Buddha Cat rose to attention.

"A Buddha?" Maggie said squinting. "That's intriguing."

They both turned at the sound of the shop bell. It was Thursday and here was Walter, right on schedule. Tia slipped Buddha into the pocket of her apron as Cat watched intently.

"Afternoon Walter," Maggie said.

Tia moved toward the lilies and collected a handful of them. Walter had become a regular more than a year ago when his beloved wife had passed away. The lilies were for her, being the flowers Walter had brought to her on their first date all those years ago. Even now he was dressed in the formal style of a different era as he pulled money from a vest pocket and paid for the flowers he would lay on his wife's gravesite.

"Have you noticed?" Maggie said to Walter with a gesture. "We have ourselves a new shop cat apparently."

Walter bent and took Cat in. "Well hello lucky cat. You get to work with my two most favorite people in the whole world."

Welcomed in this way by Tia, Maggie and Walter, Cat experienced a sense of belonging to which he had long been a stranger.

"Does he come from a shelter?" Walter asked.

"I found him wandering the street," Tia told him.

"I'm glad he doesn't have to be alone anymore," Walter said, not wanting to leave the warmth of the shop and the company of friends.

"Actually, he wasn't alone when I found him." She reached into her apron pocket and handed Buddha to Walter. "He had this with him."

Cat padded over and threaded himself through Walter's legs.

"You're a wise cat then!" Walter said looking down.

Maggie moved toward Walter to get a better look at Buddha. "He's a little worse for wear, but look; there's a metal loop on the top of his head."

She moved her cupped hand forward and Walter placed Buddha into it.

"I think I know what to do with this little guy," she said holding Buddha up. "Stay right here."

Maggie went into the back room and scanned the shelves that held the spools of fabric they used to wrap their bouquets with. She unfolded a step stool, climbed up and began rummaging through the vast collection of ribbons. "Ah. Found it!" She pulled out a small cardboard tube wrapped with delicate black silk. "This is perfect." She stepped off the stool and went back into the shop. Opening the drawer below the cash register, she took out a pair of scissors. Then she rejoined the others.

This was the hour when the afternoon sunshine washed over the cut roses by the front window, releasing their sweet fragrance throughout the store.

"Since our cat doesn't have a tag, why doesn't he wear this?" She cut a small length of the black silk and threaded it through the loop on Buddha's head. Then she went to her knees and moved towards Cat. Cat, relieved to be near Buddha again, came forward and nuzzled Buddha with the top of his head.

"For a while there I thought I'd lost you," he said to Buddha.

"I don't think we'll be having that problem anymore," Buddha replied.

Maggie slipped the silk cord around Cat's neck and tied it just so. Not too tight, not too loose. She then adjusted it so that Buddha rested gently against Cat's chest.

"It's Cat and Buddha!" Walter exclaimed. "How wonderful!"

What was this strange sensation? Cat's heart began to throb. His realized his little seed of hope was at last taking root.

Just then the shop bell rang and a young woman with two small children came in.

Right behind them was a deliveryman pushing a handcart piled with boxes of fresh cut sunflowers. Suddenly the shop was in full swing and a bit crowded.

Walter bent down and pet Cat one last time. "Guess I'll be seeing you next week," he said. Then he straightened and held out his hands to Tia and Maggie, who each took one.

"Ladies, always a pleasure," he said. And with that he left with his lilies.

Maggie and Tia turned to the business at hand and so Cat took the opportunity to seek out the afternoon sunshine. He hopped up onto the window ledge at the front of the shop, where it was bright and warm and comfortable. He walked three full circles before lowering himself down.

Just before he sank into the most peaceful nap of his life he rubbed his chin against Buddha. There were no words between Cat and Buddha then. Just peace. And ease. And joy.

Yes, this would do. They were home.

Printed in Great Britain
by Amazon

43403970R00071